# What You Want

Kimberly Smith

ISBN: 1986154300
ISBN-13: 978-1986154307

# CONTENTS

# Prologue

Maximilian Jackson Quinn sat in his chair at the head of the conference table. Although there was a magnificent view of Dallas from any of the windows looking down on the city, he was looking at the occupants of the other seats around the large oval-shaped table. His sister Elizabeth sat beside him on the left. Hank Wade, his lawyer, and friend sat to his right. They were waiting for him to reply to the request made by Peter Albrecht, the man sitting on the other side of his sister.

Max had sat at the head of this table for many meetings just like this one. As the head of a multi-billion-dollar company, he always sat in his comfortable black leather chair negotiating deals to get what he wanted. Under most circumstances by the time they got to this table in his suite of offices high above downtown Dallas, he had already won. Today was different. His opposition had come to the table with conditions that he was holding on to fervently.

Peter Albrecht was the owner of Albrecht Armor, a security software firm that had created one of the best computer security products on the market. It was a small company, not publicly traded and therefore not as well-known as many of the others who dominated the market. Max saw the potential of the company and knew that it could become a contender and maybe even dominate the market. He wanted this company's product, and until this moment he had been sure it was his for the taking. They had come to an agreement on the sale price, but Mr. Albrecht stated a condition for sale and was holding firm on it.

Max already knew the history of the company. Peter's son had started the business and had been in the process of taking it public when he and his mother died in a tragic car accident. Mr. Albrecht took ownership of the company, but his heart wasn't in it. He wanted to retire to Florida, but before he would sign this deal, he had stipulated that he wanted to ensure that the employees of the company would not be laid off or fired upon transfer of ownership. Mr. Albrecht knew Max's history as well.

Max had been sitting quietly, thinking for a few moments, when his sister turned to him. He knew what she expected him to say. She and Hank would expect him to tell Mr. Albrecht that he would not make that promise. In all the years they had been in business Max had never hesitated to make a decision and stick to it. Beth looked past her brother to Hank, who gave a slight rise in his eyebrows indicating that he had no idea what was going on.

Max remembered a conversation he'd had recently with his grandpa Jack. His grandfather had expressed his concern over some of Max and Beth's business dealings. He had accused them of being coldhearted and forgetting about the little people. Max hadn't thought anything of it and told his grandfather that he was making the best choices for his business.

His grandfather, a very outspoken man, told him exactly what was on his mind. "I'm concerned about the kind of man you're becoming. You've taken a company that I started years ago and turned it into a hugely successful business. Max, I think that you've lost touch with reality. You've never wanted for anything. It's the reason you don't understand what the average person has to go through to survive in this economy. You buy companies and break them into pieces. Every time you do that you affect the lives of the people that are let go from these jobs. Have you ever thought about it from their point of view? I brought your father into the business, and I don't regret that, He's shrewd, and he has taught you everything he knows, but sometimes he could be cold-blooded, and I don't want you to look back at your life and realize that you could have done things better.

You were born into a life where you have never had to decide which bill gets paid and which one waits until you have the money, but not everyone has it like that. Just think about the choices you're making. I know you're thinking of the company's bottom line but take some consideration for the lives you're affecting.

His grandpa was right. His father had taken over the business from grandpa Jack, and he taught Max and Beth to do whatever it took to get what they wanted to expand the business. Growing their business is what Max had done, and now they were billionaires.

His grandfather was always talking to him and Beth about making smart choices. Max usually passed it off as just being the thoughts of an old man who was contemplating his existence in the world, but lately, Max had been wondering what his real purpose in life was. Something was compelling about Mr. Albrecht and his request. "Beth, Hank, would you give me a moment alone with Mr. Albrecht?"

While they both gave him a look of confusion, they agreed and rose from the table. Mr. Albrecht's lawyer left the room as well. Once they had closed the door behind them, Max stood and went to sit in the chair turning it to face Mr. Albrecht. Before he could say anything, Mr. Albrecht spoke, "Mr. Quinn, I know how you operate. I've done my research as well. You want the coding, the software. You will let every one of the employees go that don't write code and maybe even the ones who do once you have what you want.

I wonder if you have ever considered how the choices that you make affect the workers that you let go. These people are not just numbers on a spreadsheet. They have families to support, mortgages to pay, and many of them are living from payday to payday. If you let them go, they will be struggling to survive until they can find another job. These people were like family to my son and me as well. They have worked tirelessly, and I can't let that all be in vain. If you do not agree to my terms, then I will not sell the company."

Max leaned back in the chair, rubbing his bearded chin. He took a deep breath. The company had twenty-three employees total. There were five coders, four customer service agents, three salespeople, one account payable person, one account receivable person, one secretary, one receptionist and the lawyer. Mr. Albrecht was correct. He wanted the software, and once he had it, he had every intention of letting the workers go.

He was also correct in the fact that Max and his sister never considered what the released employees would have to face in their personal lives. "I cannot guarantee that I will keep all of the employees, but perhaps I can find places for most of them within my organization, but it will be up to me to decide who stays and who is let go."

"With all due respect, you don't know these people. How can you make an informed choice?"

Max thought for a moment before speaking. "I will evaluate them myself. I will get to know them, and I will listen to recommendations that you make."

"What do you have in mind," Mr. Albrecht asked quietly?

"Well, I don't want them to know what I'm doing. I want them to show me who they are without knowing that they are being evaluated, so you won't be able to disclose this information to them." Max remembered that there was an open position in the company as an office manager. "We will tell them I'm the new office manager. I will spend a month working with them and getting to know them before I make my decisions. That position is still open, correct?"

"Yes, it is."

"We will delay the sale for thirty days to determine if some or all of your employees can be transitioned into jobs at Q.E. For those who can't, I will provide a compensation package of fifty percent of their yearly salary. That's more than fair."

Mr. Albrecht thought for a moment. He knew it was a good deal, better than he had hoped for at any rate. "We have a deal."

Max stood and extended his hand to Mr. Albrecht who also stood and shook his hand. He then went to the conference room door and asked everyone to come back in. Once they were all seated again, Max outlined the deal he and Mr. Albrecht had made. Hank would draw up the new contract and once it was signed Max would begin his evaluations. At the end of the thirty days, they would finalize their deal and Max would have what he wanted.

Hank offered to walk Mr. Albrecht and his attorney to the elevator. Max grabbed his things and headed to his office with Beth following behind him. Once they were enclosed behind the solid wooden doors she spoke, "What are you doing?"

Max sat his things on his desk and then moved to the bar and poured two glasses of champagne. He handed one to her and raised his glass. "Getting what I want." Beth touched her glass to his, and they sipped the cool golden liquid. "He wants to protect his people and what we may have to pay out to do that, is a small price for what we are getting in return."

"Why the evaluations? Even though I don't like the idea of this compensation package, we could easily afford to offer that and move on without taking a month to play undercover boss." Beth asked, moving to sit in one of the chairs in front of his desk.

Max moved to the big leather chair behind his desk resting his free hand on the top of it. "I don't think he would have gone for it. He took over this business after his son died and had kept it profitable enough to pay the workers. I think he did it out of love for his son and what his son would want him to do." Max turned to the window swallowing the last of his champagne, "Maybe it's just time to do things differently."

"So, you've grown a conscience." She said finishing her drink before rising from her chair to place the glass on the bar and leaving the room. She knew her brother well. She also knew that their grandfather had been chatting with him recently as he had with her.

She knew that Max would keep his word. Not one of the employees would be released without either being offered a job in Quinn Enterprises or receiving a compensation package to see them through finding new employment. Her brother had a reputation for getting what he wanted, but he was a man of his word.

After Beth left his office, he expected Hank to come asking questions, but he didn't. Instead, he asked Max to meet him at a bar in uptown after work for a drink. He and Hank had been friends since childhood, and since college, they had been planning and working together to build their empire. They worked well together, so Max was not surprised when after their second drink Hank asked, "What is going on with you Max?"

Max set his glass down and looked Hank in the eye. "Nothing really," he paused. "I had a conversation with my grandfather and..." he hesitated.

"He got to you, got in your head," Hank said swallowing the last of his beer.

"He just got me to thinking about what all this means. You know what kind of person am I?"

"It means that you have worked hard to build this company, to become a success. You are one of the most eligible bachelors in the country. You date hot women and have more money than most people can fathom."

"Don't forget, I'm extremely handsome too," Max said laughing.

Hank laughed too. "Yes, there is that as well, although you are not as handsome as I am. I get it. You're contemplating your life and the meaning of it all. I've been doing the same thing lately."

Max rubbed his chin. "What are your conclusions?"

"I think grandpa Jack would say that our survival instincts are kicking in. We have the means to support a family, and it's time to settle down." Hank said paraphrasing Max's grandfather.

"You think this is about settling down and our desire to reproduce?"

"I do."

Max stared at Hank for a minute. Hank hadn't been acting like his usual self. He was always talking about the latest young woman he was seeing and jetting off for the weekend with some young beauty queen, but then so was he. Lately, Hank disappeared and spent a lot of time quietly texting someone on his phone. It suddenly dawned on Max; Hank was in love.

"Who is she," Max asked?

Hank shook his head. "No one I want to discuss."

"I'm not stupid, a little slow on this one, but not stupid. You are involved with someone, and from your reaction, this woman is not just a passing fancy."

Hank twirled the bottle around peeling the label off. "There is someone, but I'm not sure she feels the same about me as I do about her."

"You're kidding me, right? There is a woman in this city who isn't begging to be in your bed, let alone visualizing being your wife?" Max chuckled.

"Don't laugh. This one is different. Not only is the lady beautiful, but she is also smart and successful," Hank paused. "Also, she is not making this easy for me, and somewhere out there is a woman who is going to grab your heart and twist it into a knot. I will be there when that day comes my friend." Hank smiled at him and winked an eye. "Enough talk about women, how do you plan to go to work at Albrecht Armor without being recognized?"

Hank had a point. He was often in tech magazines, and since dating and breaking up with Teegan Reelz, model and up and coming actress, he regularly appeared in tabloid magazines. Max would need to go undercover to ensure that no one knew him. "Well, I was thinking of coloring my hair and shaving," he said rubbing his chin again. Beyond that, Max hadn't given it much thought, but Hank had a point. He and Hank discussed what he could do to change his look. He figured he would tone down his clothing and hopefully no one would know who he was.

Hank's phone beeped and buzzed a few times while they were discussing his new look. Max realized it was the woman Hank was seeing because the smile Hank displayed while reading the message was unlike anything he'd seen on his face when he received business messages. "Go man, go to your woman," Max said signaling the waitress to settle their tab.

Hank gave him a bro hug and left the bar.

# Chapter 1 Jackson's First Day

Victoria Timmons looked from her boss to the man standing at his side. She took a deep breath, forced a smile on her face and extended her hand to the stranger. "Welcome to Albrecht Armor." His hand was warm, and she felt a tingle run up her spine when he touched her. As she let his hand go, she looked at Peter, who had turned away from her and would not meet her gaze.

"Will you show Jackson to his office and help him get settled? I've already given him the security codes and keys to the building."

Although he phrased it as a question, Victoria knew Peter was not asking. "Of course, I will. Mr. Coates, will you allow me a moment alone with Peter?" She asked in a friendly tone.

"Only if you will call me Jackson." The man said smiling at her before leaving the room.

Victoria watched him leave and spoke as soon as the door closed. "Peter, what is this? I thought that..."

Peter interrupted her, "I know what you thought." He sighed heavily before meeting her eyes with his own. "I can't tell you how sorry I am about this, but I hired Jackson for the office manager's position, and I need you to trust me and that decision. I need you to show him the ropes and be his right hand until he's up to speed on everything. Will you do that for me?"

Victoria said nothing for a moment. She could tell that this decision was not something he had come to lightly. When he stepped in to take over the company after the death of his son, she had trusted him then, and for the past year, he had done a great job running the business. "I will." I'm just not happy about it she added silently.

She exited the office to find her new boss leaning against the wall with his arms casually folded over his broad chest. "Follow me," she said as she passed him.

Jackson fell in line behind her. As he had leaned against the wall waiting for her to come out, he chuckled at the look on her face when Peter introduced them. She had come into the room smiling and happy. The file he had on her and the other employees did not contain photos, but the image in his head did not match up with who Victoria turned out to be. She was attractive, tall and curvy with flawless milk chocolate skin, expressive amber colored eyes outlined with thick, long lashes, high cheekbones, and bow-shaped full lips. It didn't appear that Victoria wore much makeup and she didn't need to. Her hair was pulled back in a knot at the nape of her neck; It seemed to be wavy or maybe curly. She wore black slacks, white button-down with a black sweater. Her outfit was boring, dull and off the rack and not from a known designer. She would look great in red and found himself picturing her in a dress or skirt to show off her curves.

She walked quickly from Peters office, pointing out where the conference room, break room and restrooms were. When they were in the open-air area, she explained that it was where everyone else worked. She didn't bother to introduce him to the others who stared as she led him across the room to the only other walled in office. She opened the door and flipped the light switch, bathing the room in light. "This is your office."

He walked passed her surveying the room. It was a typical office space with a large desk, computer, phone system, and the necessary basic supplies. There were a couple of file cabinets and shelves.

Victoria followed Jackson's gaze to the supply shelf. "Unfortunately, we keep the office supplies in here, so you will be visited from time to time. Angela, your predecessor, had an open-door policy and she kept the door open."

Jackson noticed that she seemed to force the word predecessor. "That's great, I will follow in that tradition." He moved to the desk to sit down.

"I will have one of the programmers set up your log in information as soon as possible," she said moving around to stand next to him. She leaned past him to turn on the system and entered her name and password. "For now, you can use mine."

She smelled like flowers. It was a gentle scent. "When will I meet the other employees?"

Victoria opened her email application, and there was a new email from Peter announcing a town hall meeting in half an hour. "I guess you will be meeting them at the town hall that Peter has just set up."

Jackson watched her as she moved towards the door. "Aren't you afraid I may read your email?"

Victoria stopped looking over her shoulder with a smile. "No, in fact, I expect you to do just that. I'll be right back to get your training started," she said and left the office.

Victoria walked quickly into the lady's room entering a stall. She didn't have to go; she just needed a moment to deal with her feelings. She was upset. Peter had promised her this position if she proved herself and she felt she had done just that. How could he bring in an outsider and now she was expected to train him? As her eyes became watery, she realized she was hurt. She felt cheated. The outer door opened.

"Vicky, I know you are in here," Sasha said as she closed the door.

Victoria took a deep breath, taking a bit of tissue and dabbing her eyes. She flushed the tissue and came out of the stall. "What's up Sasha?"

"Who's the hot nerd?" Sasha stood leaning against the sink, "He looks familiar to me.

Victoria stood next to her washing her hands. "The new office manager."

"Wait, What?" Sasha said turning to look at her in the mirror.

"You heard me." Victoria grabbed a paper towel and dried her hands.

"I thought you were going to get promoted."

Victoria smoothed her hair. "Yeah, well apparently that's not the plan." She moved around Sasha to the door.

"Okay, so who is this guy?" Sasha asked before she could open the door.

"Hell, if I know." Victoria opened the door and walked to her cubicle grabbing several of the manuals that contained the processes and procedures. Sasha took her seat across from Victoria's and put on her headset getting ready to answer calls as they came in.

Victoria smiled at her and carried the manuals into Jackson's office. She placed them on his desk with a thud. "You may want to familiarize yourself with these. They are the processes and procedures we currently have in place. Each one is labeled." She ran through them quickly, "finance, sales, programming and product testing, customer and tech support, and general office. I think this is a good place for you to start. The phone is labeled with everyone's extension if you need me just push the button marked Vicky."

Before she could exit the room, he asked, "Do you prefer being called Vicky or Victoria?"

Everyone had always shortened her name to Vicky. Her mother, her friends, and her coworkers all called her Vicky. No one had ever asked her which she preferred. "You can call me Victoria." She said smiling with emphasis on 'You' and left his office.

She sat down at her desk and looked at her calendar to see what she was supposed to handle today. The impromptu town hall would push everything back which meant something was going to go undone unless she worked late. She did not want to spend the night in the office. She had worked her part-time job all weekend, and she wanted just to go home and chill-out.

Her phone buzzed indicating that she had a new text message. She slid her phone out of her pocket and read the message.

Sasha: Is he single?

Everyone in the office communicated using the office instant messenger and knew it was recorded. Sasha and Victoria sent personal messages via cell phone.

Victoria: I don't know. I'm gonna tell Brian.

Brian was Sasha's husband. He and Sasha had been happily married for some time which meant that Sasha was hoping to fix someone up and Victoria prayed it wasn't her.

Sasha: Not for me. Jessica wants to know.

Jessica worked in the finance department handling accounts payable. She was single and always looking for a man.

Sasha: Laura and Sam want to know as well. LOL

Victoria snorted as she read the last text. Laura was their best salesperson, and Sam was the other member of her team.

Victoria: Wow, the guy isn't here an hour yet
and everyone wants him, and he's not all that.

Sasha: Are you blind? He's geeky and gorgeous.

Victoria checked the time on her phone. It was nearly time for the Town Hall. She quickly sent the receptionist Millie a message to set the phones to night mode. She also sent two group messages, one asking for a volunteer to man the tech and customer support lines during the meeting. Sasha volunteered. She also sent one to everyone that they should go to the conference room for the meeting.

As everyone headed towards the conference room, Victoria went to Jackson's office. She watched him for a few seconds from the door. He was attractive in a nerdy sort of way. He was reading one of the manuals. His light brown hair lay messily on his head, slightly curling on the ends. She couldn't see his eyes well the way he had his head bent, but she knew they were a light blue. His lips had that healthy pink color, and his bottom one was full and sensuous. He had a strong jawline and straight nose. You could also see that he had a great body underneath the dorky plaid shirt and khaki pants and he was tall. She, at five feet eight inches tall, had to look up to meet his eyes when they met.

She had been standing there watching him for a minute when he raised his head to look at her. "It's time for the meeting," she said hoping he hadn't been aware that she was watching him. He was aware she realized. It was the way he smiled when their eyes met, that gave him away. She rolled her eyes slightly, turned walking away.

He had sensed her presence the moment she stopped in the doorway to his office. He knew she was looking at him and he recognized that he liked it. He followed her to the conference room. All the seats were taken. Victoria found a spot on the wall near the door. Jackson followed and stood next to her brushing her shoulder with his arm. She moved away from him just a bit so that they were no longer touching. A few minutes later Peter entered and went to stand at the head of the table.

Peter looked at Victoria and smiled. "Thanks for dropping everything to attend this town hall meeting. I'm sure that you all have noticed a new face in the office today. I have finally filled Angela's position. Jackson Coates comes to us with an abundance of experience." Everyone in the room turned to look a Jackson, who raised his hand to wave and glance around the room. "Vicky will be helping him to get up to speed on everything he needs to know, but I'm sure he will be meeting with all of you at some point. Please help make his transition a successful one. Jackson, would you like to say anything?"

Jackson smiled and stepped forward, "Thanks, Peter. I just want to say that I'm happy to be here and I will be speaking with you all soon to get a better understanding of who you are and what you do so that we can work together to make Albrecht Armor more successful than it already is."

Peter spoke again, "Victoria will work up a schedule for each of you to meet with Jackson, so send her your availability by close of business today. Alright everyone, let's get back to work."

Victoria bit her lip to hold in her frustration. Not only was she to teach him how to do his job, but she was to act as his secretary too. She filed out of the room with the others but went to the break room instead of returning to her desk. She grabbed an empty mug and poured some coffee. As she was adding cream and sugar, Jessica, Sam, and Laura surrounded her.

Victoria looked up surveying all their faces. They were eager to ask questions. "I don't know anything about him," she said taking a sip of her coffee.

"Nothing?" Sam asked with disbelief. "Peter doesn't do anything without you knowing about it. You don't know anything?"

"Nothing more than his name and apparently Peter doesn't include me in everything." Victoria said looking at the three of them. "You will all have the chance to ask him questions when I set your appointments with him," she added with a bit of attitude and left the room.

Before she went back to her desk to tell Sasha what happened in the meeting, she spoke with Tanner, her head programmer. "Tanner, can you set up Jackson's login credentials and give him Angela's laptop?" Angela had always had a laptop available to her, though she hardly ever used it. Somehow, she sensed that Jackson would put his to good use.

Tanner winked at her, "Of course, Vicky." Victoria patted his shoulder and walked back to her desk. Victoria stood next to Sasha's desk giving her the summary of the meeting as Sasha flipped through TechEn, an entertainment and technology magazine.

"What are you reading?" Victoria asked her, pushing the cover so that she could see it better.

"Some magazine I found on Eugene's desk. It's all tech, geek, gaming stuff." Sasha said flipping pages. "Maybe you'll be featured in a magazine like this one day."

"I thought you planned to get me married and producing a bunch of kids."

"That was the plan, but you keep messing it up. I think that the average man isn't what you need. Maybe I need to find you a high-powered businessman, Like this guy." She said showing her a page of the magazine.

Victoria took a quick look at the picture. "I don't think so. I don't do beards."

"Look past the beard," Sasha said looking at the picture again. "Those eyes, those lips, those bank accounts." She said laughing at the end. "He's hot."

Sam slid over in his chair, looking at the magazine after hearing the mention of a hot man. "Who is hot?" Sam fanned himself. "Oh, this is the guy that dated Teegan Reelz. They looked yummy together." Sam pulled the magazine from Sasha's hand and rolled back to his desk as her phone signaled she had a customer call.

Victoria spent the better part of the morning arranging appointment times for everyone in the office. The things she intended to work on would be pushed to later in the day. She took a few customer service calls when Sam and Sasha were on calls already. Victoria's primary job when she had been hired was to handle the email support, but now she did a lot more. Just before noon, her desk phone chirped. It was

Jackson. She picked it up, but before she could speak, he summoned her. "Come see me."

She looked at the receiver and then towards his office. He was going to be that kind of boss. He got off on making demands and having power. She sent Sasha an instant message through the office system that she would be in Jackson's office for a few minutes and to decide where they were going for lunch.

Sasha gave her a strange look over the cubicle wall. They usually only went out for lunch on Friday. It was what Victoria called her cheat day. She cheated on the never-ending diet and spent some of the extra money she earned from her second job. It was Monday and eating out on Monday was unusual, but Sasha also knew how hard Victoria had been working to prove to Peter that she could do everything in the office so that he would promote her and give her a raise. She understood that today was an exception to the rule.

As Victoria entered the office, Jackson spoke without raising his head from the manual he was reviewing. "Close the door." Victoria closed the door and crossed the room to his desk.

"Sit down," he said closing the manual and finally looking at her. He had read the first few manuals. They were well written and very detailed. "I noticed that there are no notes about who wrote them or when. I assume that the previous office manager created this." He said tapping the customer support manual.

"Is there a problem with them?" He seemed surprised by the quality of the contents. Victoria figured that he was going to want to revamp or maybe create new manuals.

"No problem, just that they should be dated, and the author should have put their name on them so that we can track the creation of the documents as well as the changes. Do you know when they were created?"

"Yes, they were created by me after Angela left the company," Victoria said sitting up a little straighter noting the surprise on Jackson's face. "You looked shocked."

"It's just that the company has been in business for several years and you have only been here for the last two. Documents like this should have existed from the beginning of the company."

Victoria noted that he knew exactly how long she had been working there. She guessed that Peter must have given him that information. "Angela was great with people, but she was not one for putting chaos into order. I don't like chaos. I like order. I started standardizing how we do things with her blessing, and when people were hired, I trained them to ensure that we do all our jobs the same way. That's how the documents were created. I didn't feel the need to put my name on anything, and I never thought to put the date anywhere since I keep a copy of each file on the company server with the dates that they are created and version numbers as they are updated."

"You, created the customer support manuals?" Jackson asked smiling at her. He was impressed. "Who created the other manuals?"

"I created them all, and I work closely with everyone here to keep them updated." She said proudly. She met his eyes. He said nothing for a moment, and then he slowly smiled at her. "Why are you looking at me like that?"

"I'm not easily impressed Victoria." he said smiling at her and added, "I may have found a diamond in the rough."

What did he mean by that Victoria wondered? "Sorry to interrupt," Sasha said knocking and pushing the door open.

"Victoria and I are going to Hop-daddy's for lunch. Several others are joining us. We wanted to see if you would come too. We'd like to welcome you to the company."

Jackson looked at his watch. He hadn't realized it was time for lunch already. "I'm starving. That would be nice." Going with them would give him the opportunity to find out personally who everyone was.

"Great, I'll round everyone up, and we will head out when you're ready," Sasha said before closing the door.

Once the door closed, Victoria spoke, "You don't have to go with us." Victoria added, "I mean if you have plans already."

"I don't have plans." Jackson smiled brightly. It was obvious that she didn't want him to join them. Except when he was praising her work, she had been acting as if she didn't like him. "We can continue discussing these manuals after lunch." He rose and walked around the desk. "Shall we?"

Victoria rose and led the way out of his office. The others, Jessica, Laura, Sam, Sasha, Tanner, George, Millie, and Peter, were waiting near the entrance. Peter and Tanner both had large SUV's, so everyone piled into one or the other of their vehicles. Victoria, still being a little angry with Peter chose to ride with Tanner's group. She slid into the back seat behind the driver's seat.

Jackson waited as the others piled into the cars. Since Victoria was the only person he had met and talked to, he watched to see who she was riding with and he chose to go in the car with her. Just as she was reaching for the door handle to close the door, he grabbed the door and smiled at her. She frowned but slid to the center of the back seat. He closed the door throwing his arm over the back of the seat, which wedged her body against his. From hip to thigh they touched even as she pressed her legs together. Millie got in on the other side of Victoria. Tanner and Sasha sat in the front.

Victoria shifted her leg, trying to move away from Jackson. His arm was resting on the back of the seat touching her shoulders. Sitting next to him was a little too close for her comfort. Heat rolled off his body making her feel very warm, especially where their bodies touched. Thankfully the ride to the restaurant was not too long. Tanner let them out near the door. "I'll see you inside as soon as I find a parking space."

Once they were all inside the hostess led them to a long table near the front window. Jackson noticed that Victoria placed herself between Millie and Sasha at the end away from him. He quickly found himself the focus of attention from Jessica and Laura, who sat on either side of him.

Jessica worked in the finance department doing accounts payable work. She was in her late twenties and was single with no kids. She was an attractive woman with blonde hair that hung to her shoulders split down the middle with perfect highlights that could only come from a salon. She had almond-shaped ocean blue eyes. Jessica's make up looked light and natural, but he learned while dating the model that makeup could be heavily applied and still look natural.

Laura who bragged to him about being the best sales rep at the company was also attractive. She was in her thirties, she told him. She tossed her long dark hair frequently and licked her dark red lips at him as they chatted. She continued to touch his hand and arm every chance she got. He was polite to her and Jessica both, but Victoria drew his attention. She, Millie and Sasha were talking among themselves. She smiled a lot. Her face lit up, occasionally she looked his way, and the smile would fade.

Throughout lunch, he talked to everyone close to him, and a realized that Victoria influenced every part of the business in some way. She provided feedback to the support teams from surveys she conducted with their customers to improve their service. Victoria also handled reviews on the product and presented that information to the programmers. She worked closely with the sales team to help them flesh out potential customers. It seemed there was a lot to Victoria and he intended to find out everything.

He knew he was staring at her, but he couldn't help himself. He liked looking at her, and he noticed that of the women at the table she was the only one having a hearty meal. She was eating a burger and fries. The other's seemed far too concerned with their waistlines. They were eating salads and wraps or grilled chicken. He'd had enough of that dating the model. She never ate more than a bite or two of anything.

Sasha leaned closer to Victoria. "He's looking at you again," she whispered.

Victoria involuntarily glanced in Jackson's direction. He smiled. She turned her eyes to Sasha. "So what?"

Millie who had leaned closer to hear, spoke. "Maybe he wants to get his swirl on." She and Sasha giggled like teenagers. Victoria rolled her eyes.

"What am I going to do with you two?" Victoria said dipping one of her fries in the ketchup on her plate. "He probably wishes he could get away from Jessica and Laura. I'm sure they are both plotting how long before they will get him to bed. I bet that Jessica will get him before Laura."

"No way," Millie said. "Look at the way Laura is pawing him. I'm betting on her."

"Both of you are wrong," Sasha said after sipping her glass of tea. "I'm betting on Vicky."

"I'm not in the race," Victoria said before biting her burger.

Sasha smiled and pushed Victoria with her shoulder. "You

are in the race whether you want to be or not. Look at how he reacts every time Laura touches him. You almost see his skin crawling, not to mention he is looking at you again."

She finished her burger and wiped her mouth. Jackson wasn't interested in her, and she was not interested in him. It was taking everything good in her just to be nice to him since he had taken her job away from her.

Sasha was always trying to fix Victoria up with someone. This situation was no different. Sasha thought every one of her single friends needed to be fixed up with someone. Victoria had been out with her and her husband and some friend or family member so many times that Sasha had said she had run out of guys for her, which was okay with Victoria.

She didn't have time for dating or a relationship. Her hands were full trying to get ahead at work and taking care of her mother and the house, she had just bought.

Victoria glanced around the table, George was looking at her. She smiled at him. George was sweet, and if he were older, she would have said yes when he asked her out months ago. He was quiet and smart. Victoria like men that were tall and looked like they were sculpted with a chisel and hammer. George was thin and even in flats she looked down at him when they stood face to face.

After he started to work at Albrecht Armor, he would leave little gifts on her desk, things like the coffee mug that had become her favorite. It said, 'Have you tried turning it off and on again?' It had been sitting on her desk filled with candy one morning when she came in. It had taken a while before she found out that George was the one to give it to her.

She had also received a mouse pad that said 'Teamwork - A group of people doing what I say.' There were many other things left on her desk before she realized that they were from George. They had been working late to cover the phones. He had offered to lock up the building. Victoria had gotten all the way to her car and realized that her cell phone was still in her desk drawer. She came in just as he was setting a beautiful glass candy dish on her desk filled with snickers bites, her favorite candy.

He blushed and finally told her that he thought she was beautiful and asked her to go out with him. Victoria sighed thinking about it. She explained to him that he was much too young for her and that she was flattered. He took it well, and he still left gifts on her desk occasionally.

# Chapter 2 A Mother's Advice

By the time Victoria parked her car under the carport in her driveway, she was mentally exhausted. She spent the afternoon, working with Tanner on the proposed changes to the software and producing reports from the survey information she had received last Friday. The manuals she had given Jackson kept him busy enough that she didn't have to spend too much more time with him today.

Victoria crossed the living room and set her things in her bedroom before heading to her mother's room in the back of the house. "Momma. I'm home."

"Hey, Vicky baby. How was work?" She hugged her mother who sat about two feet from the television in her favorite armchair. Helen Timmons had been legally blind since Victoria had been a child. She had almost no vision in one eye and very limited vision in the other.

She had never thought of herself as handicapped. She had worked for more than thirty years at the Dallas Lighthouse for the Blind, a factory that produced pencils, binders, brooms and mops and a host of other things under government contracts. She cooked and cleaned and did most things like everyone else. She even encouraged Victoria at eighteen to move out and live on her own. If you didn't know her personally, you might not realize that she had almost no vision. She had retired a few years before and quickly realized that the checks she received from Social Security were not enough to cover her expenses.

Victoria allowed her mother the independence Helen wanted until it was clear that she could no longer afford to live by herself. Victoria purchased the house they now lived in and told her mother that the only way they both were going to be alright is if they lived together. She tried not to burden her mother with anything. It had always been tight financially, but her mother's health was deteriorating, and she needed more medications and had frequent visits to the doctor.

Victoria had found a second job that allowed her to make extra cash and control her schedule, so she could work when she wanted to. A few nights a week and sometimes on the weekend she worked as a delivery driver for Favor. She ran errands and picked up food and groceries for others. It was convenient and easy, and she got paid quickly. She was doing all she could to take care of the two of them and had hoped this promotion would provide more money so that she could give up her second job.

"We'll talk about it later," Victoria said with a sigh.

Victoria started out the room. "Have you had dinner? I think I'll order pizza."

"No, I haven't."

After having a shower and getting comfy in her favorite sweats, she placed an order for pizza and sat in the white leather chair putting her feet up on the ottoman. She sunk in the soft leather and closed her eyes. She couldn't stop thinking about her new boss and how strangely Peter was behaving today. After lunch, she went to his office to speak with him. She knocked on his open door. "You got a minute?"

"Sure," he said waving her in.

Victoria closed the door behind her and crossed the room. She could see that Peter looked stressed. "Tell me what's going on. I'm not the only one who has noticed that you're behaving oddly."

Peter sighed heavily. He knew that he could not legally say

anything. The contract for the sale of the company had an airtight confidentiality clause in it. "Vicky," He paused indicating that she should sit down. Once she sat, he looked her in the eye. "I'm sorry that I gave you hope that you would be replacing Angela. At the time I believed that it would work out. Unfortunately, I had to make a different choice.

You have a lot of potential. You're great with the customers, you've organized all the departments, and you do so much around here. I think that you need to focus on one thing." He had planned to sell the business all along, but once he got to know these people he wanted to make sure they would be alright when he did.

"What's that?" She asked.

Peter smiled, and it wasn't the smile she usually saw. This one didn't reach his eyes. "Right now, assisting Jackson with getting acclimated to his position. Show him who you are, who we are as a company and why we are the best at what we do."

She had returned to her desk still confused and angry. It seemed that she would never get ahead. She thought things would be different at Albrecht Armor. She was getting in on the ground floor of what had the potential to be a big business. At every company she had worked for, she got pigeon hold in a job and never seriously considered for advancement. She had always gotten passed over when she applied for a better position, and it was happening again. She should update her resume and start sending them out. Maybe she had gotten all she could from this job, and it was time to move on.

She spent the rest of the afternoon analyzing the raw data from her surveys and getting the reports ready for the next day's meeting with each department to go over her findings. She tried her best to ignore Jackson after he strode out of his office and announced that he wanted to sit in on some customer calls. She set him up to sit with Sasha first and then with Sam. "Will I get the chance to sit with you as well?" he asked her as she found a headset for him.

"No, I'm afraid I have to catch up on all the other things that have gotten pushed around by your," she paused, "surprised appearance." She tried to sound sweet.

Jackson chuckled, she was not happy with him being there, and although she had been very professional, occasionally her discontent showed.

Victoria tried to ignore his deep voice as he quietly asked Sasha and Sam questions during their calls, but it was nearly impossible. Each time he asked a question or laughed, she got goosebumps on her skin. She was also annoyed by the way Sasha and Sam seemed to be flirting with him. When he finally returned to his office, she wanted to throw something at his retreating back. Not because she didn't like him, well maybe that was part of it, but also because it seemed everyone in the office was falling under his spell.

The sound of the doorbell brought her back to the present. She put all thoughts of Jackson and Peter out of her mind and enjoyed the next few hours with her mother. They ate in the living room watching a comedy on cable. "Tell me what has my Vicky upset."

Victoria sat near her mother and then scooted over so that she could lay her head on Helen's lap.

"That bad, huh?" Helen said stroking Victoria's hair.

"Peter hired someone else for the office manager's position."

Helen continued to stroke her daughter's head. "Maybe this is a good thing."

Victoria shot up, facing her mother, "Why would you say that? I've worked my ass off to prove that I can do that and any other job there. His hiring this guy is just another example of me being passed over."

"So, you think this is because of your being black?"

Victoria sighed, she hadn't wanted to say it. "Yes, and or maybe," she stuttered in her anger. "Maybe it's because I'm not good looking."

"Bullshit." Her mother said with force.

"Come on Momma; I know that I'm not ugly, but you have to admit that certain people get ahead faster in business based on the way they look."

"Do you honestly believe that?"

"I have proof. Every time I have applied for a position that I am qualified for, someone who looks nothing like me gets it. These people are almost always thin, blonde and blue-eyed. The American ideal of beauty, yet I have to train them, and half the time I end up doing their work for them."

"Your new boss is white and attractive? Life isn't always fair Victoria Louise Timmons, but you know as well as I do that everything happens according to God's plan. This promotion may not be what he has planned for you. I assure you that if God has removed this office managers position, which is just a regular piece of meat, from the menu; that he has something better than you can imagine waiting for you. He is preparing to serve you a prime cut of meat." Her mother rose and pulled her into a tight hug. "Have faith that God, the most high, is preparing you for a feast of epic proportions."

It was no wonder that Victoria was a foodie. Her mother always calmed her down with some analogy about food. She smiled hugging her mother tighter. Her mother's faith seeped into her, but Victoria still wasn't happy about this turn of events with Jackson taking her promotion out from under her.

# Chapter 3 The Attraction

Jackson left Albrecht Armor and went to his headquarters before going home. He knew that Beth and Hank could handle anything in his absence, but he wanted to sit in his chair and be himself for a while. It was difficult pretending to be someone else, even if it was someone he had created. Beth had helped him prepare his wardrobe and style for his days undercover at Albrecht.

Things had gone well. While sitting with Sam and Sasha, he saw how effective they both were when it came to resolving issues and making the customer feel that they cared about their problems. Sam told him that their work had been okay when he first started to work for Albrecht, but they were better now because of Victoria. When Angela hired him, he hadn't been given any direction. She had just told him to resolve the issues as quickly as possible, but when Victoria started working there, she would nudge him to say certain things in different ways. It made a big difference. She eventually sat down with him and Sasha and told them 'Put yourself in the customer's shoes. How would you want someone to talk to you and to treat you if you were having this issue?"

He was surprised by the personal questions that Sasha asked. She wanted to know if he was married and when he said no, she went on to ask if he was involved with someone. He assumed she was flirting with him, but she later explained that she was married with two kids and was asking because a few single ladies and one guy in the office wanted to know. He couldn't help but laugh. He was sure that Laura was one of the ladies who wanted to know his status. He didn't need to know which guy was curious about him.

Victoria Timmons popped into his mind, and he found himself smiling. Everyone he had talked to so far in the office seemed to admire her. Jackson wondered if she were involved with anyone. She wasn't married, he had noticed that there was no ring adorning the third finger of her left hand, but that didn't mean that there wasn't a man in her life.

That was not his concern, but he was intrigued by her. She liked things orderly and neat. He noted that she kept everything on her desk placed efficiently. He like that she smelled like flowers. It was a light scent. You had to be close to her to catch a whiff of it. In the car, he had moved a little closer to inhale it again when his thigh rubbed hers. He'd felt a jolt of electricity just before she shifted her leg from his. Goosebumps formed on his arms as he thought of it. He shook his head to clear his thoughts.

Sasha had also wanted to know where he had worked before coming to Albrecht.  He hadn't considered that he would need a backstory. Jackson figured it would be best to stick close to the truth. He told her he had worked at Quinn Enterprises in the support group. She couldn't believe that he had left Q.E. to work at Albrecht. She also wanted to know why he was still single, considering that he was attractive, intelligent and straight.

She offered to introduce him to some single women if he liked. He assured her that he was not interested.  She laughed and then told him he wasn't the first person to turn down her efforts. He pushed thoughts of Albrecht and Victoria from his mind and began responding to emails and Q.E. business that required his attention.

After he got home, he ended up sitting at the desk in his home office working for a few more hours. If he thought about work, he was good, but the minute he paused, his thoughts turned to Victoria. He was interested in her, that was obvious. No matter how often he told himself it was all professional, he knew there was more to it than that.

Otherwise, he wouldn't be trying to understand why she sometimes acted as if she didn't like him.

The next morning Jackson stood in front of his bathroom mirror shaving his new growth of beard stubble. He felt naked without his beard, but Beth had said without it, he would be harder to recognize him as Maximillion Quinn, especially after they dyed his hair brown and styled it differently. It also meant he didn't have to dye his beard.

He wiped off the remnants of shaving cream, ran his hands through his now brown hair and proceeded to make himself into Jackson Coates. Before he left for work, he looked at himself once more in the mirror. He wanted to make sure that there was no trace of Maximilian Quinn. He had been careful to put away his expensive watch and signet ring. Instead, he chose a simple watch with a leather band.

He straightened the collar of his plain looking polo shirt before sliding on the eyeglass his sister had given him. When he showed her his undercover look, she told him that he still looked too much like himself. She found him a pair of wire-rimmed glasses that had ordinary glass lenses. The spectacles, darker hair and dorky clothes worked well to aid him in his disguise. He looked like someone in middle management and not the millionaire playboy that he was.

He chuckled when he grabbed the keys which were by the front door. He had nearly blown the whole charade before it started. He had given a lot of thought to his appearance, but he never once thought of the car he drove. He had several, and none of them would do for the average man. If he had shown up to his first day driving an Audi R8 or his McLaren F1, it would have been over before it began. Fortunately for Max, his grandfather kept the car, a new Ford Taurus in Max's garage and it was perfect for his undercover role. It made perfect sense to use his car since he was using his grandfather's name too.

When he arrived at the Albrecht office, there were a few cars in the parking lot. He spoke to Millie who worked the front desk. Victoria was already at her desk hard at work. She was engrossed in her computer screen and didn't see him until he was standing beside her desk. "Do you always come in early?"

She glanced up at him allowing her eyes to roam down his body slowly. "I do when getting the new boss acclimated to his job interferes with me getting my work done." She was still put out by his presence. No matter what her mother had said about this situation, she was not happy about it.

He put his hands up in surrender. "I didn't mean anything by it, and in case I didn't say it yesterday. Thank you for your sacrifice."

Now she felt like crap. She hadn't meant to be rude. Well, maybe she had, but she was also tired. She suffered from insomnia from time to time. She was always cranky when she didn't get enough sleep. "I'm sorry," she said rubbing her forehead.

Jackson smiled. "Let me get you a cup of coffee."

"No, that's the last thing I need. Thank you though." She turned back to her computer. "I just need to finish these reports before everyone gets here. I have to pass these reports out today."

"Can I help?" Jackson asked.

"Are you any good with Excel spreadsheets and making charts and graphs?" She asked looking up at him with a smile that fried his brain just a little. The only other time he had seen her smile was while talking to Sasha and Millie yesterday. When he didn't answer, she turned back to her computer. "I got it, don't worry. You can look over these to get familiar with our customer base." She said pointing to a stack of papers. "They are sales reports and contracts from the past year."

"Great." He grabbed the stack of papers and went into his office. Albrecht had some impressive corporate clients. Most mid-sized companies, but once he integrated them into Quinn Enterprises, they would have fortune five-hundred corporations as clients in no time. He listened to the staff coming in and starting their work as he reviewed the papers.

He liked the sound. It was something he didn't experience anymore. Being the chief operating officer of his company, his office was large and spacious and far removed from most of his employees. In fact, the only other office space on his floor belonged to Beth and Hank. An hour later Victoria came through his door with a laptop. "We have about an hour before your first meeting with the sales staff. That is just enough time to go through the latest sales reports that I just finished? You ready?"

Jackson tidied up the stack of papers he had been reading. "Sure."

"We'll do it in the conference room." She said turning to walk out the door. As he rose to follow her, he got a great look at her ass. Yesterday she had been wearing slacks with a sweater that hung down to her thighs, but today she was wearing a knee-length navy blue skirt with a white short-sleeved blouse. Both clung to her curvy figure causing Jackson to stare at her derriere as she walked ahead of him. His eyes traveled downward. She was wearing flats, but her legs were toned and shapely. He bit his lip as he thought of her in heels and how flattering her behind would look. He needed to get a grip on his libido.

She sat down and set up the laptop, pulling a chair closer to her for him to use. Over the next hour, she showed him the sales database and tools the team used to identify and track leads. Jackson again was impressed with her knowledge of the database and the tools used by the sales team to determine new customers. She spoke with excitement and answered each question he posed to her openly and definitively.

As Victoria went over the database, she noticed that Jackson seem distracted from time to time. When she was finishing her presentation to him, she turned to find him looking at her mouth causing her to stumble over the last of her words. The color in his cheeks gave him away as he smiled and leaned back in his chair. "What?" She asked closing the laptop.

Jackson rubbed his chin. He liked her mouth, her lips were full, her teeth straight and pearly white. He wanted to kiss her, but he couldn't and certainly couldn't say what he was thinking. During her presentation, Jackson had faded in and out. He hadn't been with anyone in a few months, and it must be getting to him. That's all this was. He needed to get laid. He was fixating on her because he found her attractive.

He turned and saw her licking her lips. The tip of pink flesh as it moved quickly between her lips sent a shockwave of desire through him. They were sitting close enough for him to smell her floral scent. He wondered where on her body it would be the strongest, her wrists, her throat or maybe the valley between her milk chocolate breasts. "It's nothing."

"If you say so," Victoria said with a little attitude. He had been staring at her through most of her presentation. He did ask a few relevant questions, but his staring made her a little uncomfortable. She grabbed the laptop, standing. "Would you like to have your meetings with Laura and Jim in here or your office?"

Jackson thought for a second, "In here. I think that would be best." The conference room provided a little bit more privacy than his office.

"Alright. I will let Jim and Laura know to come in here. If you need anything else, let me know." She turned and exited the room.

Victoria could feel his eyes on her as she walked out from the conference room. She didn't like the little bubbly feeling in her stomach. She had felt it yesterday in the car when his leg touched hers, when she turned to find him looking at her lips and now as she walked away. What was wrong with her? She got back to her desk and let Jim and Laura know to go to the conference room for their meetings. Laura was scheduled to go first.

A few minutes later Victoria watched as Laura passed her desk going to the conference room. Sasha passed Laura on her way back from the break room and stopped. "Wow, the manhunt is on."

Victoria glanced over her shoulder. She had noted that Laura was looking exceptionally well today. Her hair was in cascading waves. Laura's make up was flawless. "Face beat by Mac." She said laughing.

Sasha laughed, "Could that skirt be any shorter?"

Victoria laughed again before shooing Sasha back to her desk. She had a ton of work to do and no time to be worried about Laura's outfit. Victoria got back to handling customer emails and was so engrossed in her work that she nearly jumped out of her chair when Jackson touched her shoulder. "Are you trying to give me a heart attack?" She asked him, holding her hand to her chest.

Jackson smiled, "No. I'm sorry. I didn't mean to scare you." When she jumped, he had grabbed her by the shoulders to steady her. He had goosebumps again. He released her. "I just wanted to see if you were free for lunch."

Victoria stuttered. "Uh, well." Sasha giggled from her side of the cubicle wall, and Victoria knew Sasha was laughing at her stuttering. "I was planning to work through."

"I have some questions that only you can answer. It's on me. I'd appreciate it." He pleaded.

Sasha stood up. "Go, I can cover the email and phones until you come back. Victoria gave her a dirty look, causing Sasha to giggle again. If she said no now, she'd look like she was just mean.

"Sure." She said giving in. She retrieved her purse from her desk and followed Jackson out of the office to his car. She realized he was a gentleman as he held open the office door and then the car door for her.

Once he was behind the wheel, he asked, "Where would you like to go?"

Victoria thought for a moment, she should stay on her diet and have something light, but she would just have to throw an extra work out on her schedule this week. "Velvet Taco."

He smiled, "I don't think I've ever been there."

"You are in for a treat." She said as he started the car. Victoria gave him directions. Their office was off Central Expressway, and it only took a few minutes to get there. Along the way, Victoria noted how clean the car was. She had a theory about how people kept their vehicles. She believed that how a person treated their car directly correlated how they lived their lives. If you had a messy car, your life was probably chaotic.

This car was new, and there didn't seem to be anything personal in it. No papers stuck in the pockets of the doors, no bobbles hanging from the mirror, not even an eyeglass case with sunglasses and it had that new car smell. Either he was a super neat freak, or he had just bought the car.

Everything in her car had a designated space, and everything was in its space. She kept it neat and clean. Her life was the same way organized and simple, the way she liked it. As she noticed the supple leather seats and the navigation system among other things, she also realized that he loved all the bells and whistles, the finer things. She liked them too but couldn't always afford to have them.

When they arrived at the restaurant, Jackson needed a moment to study the menu. She pointed out her favorites. He chose to get the same things she ordered, the spicy tikka chicken taco, a side of elotes corn, a side dish of tater tots with a fried egg and a slice of their red velvet cake.

As they sat with their nearly matching order, Victoria took a moment to say grace silently. She bowed her head, and when she finished, she found Jackson watching her with a smile. "Are you very religious?"

Victoria began eating. "No, I guess you could say I'm more spiritual than religious. I don't go to church much, but I believe in God and trying to live a life that he and my mother would be proud of."

He began to eat and smiled, "What about your father? Is he proud of you?"

"My father died when I was a teenager, but I think he would be."

"I'm sorry," Jackson said noting the look of sadness on her face.

She waved her free hand at him. "Thank you, but it's no big deal. Everyone dies, but not everybody lives."

Jackson asked her about her family, her friends and by the time there were done with their food he knew that Victoria did not have a boyfriend, a fact that made him happy. She lived with her mother who could not live alone on the pittance that she received from Social Security. Victoria was an only child. He could not believe his ears when in passing, she said that she was in her forties and he told her so. She also had a part-time 'hustle' as she called it. When he asked why she was working two jobs, she said quietly, "Because I have to."

While he didn't know the specifics of her expenses, he knew that she along with the others at Albrecht were probably underpaid, by his standards anyway. Peter was paying them what he could afford to keep the business running and profitable. He wanted to ask her more questions.

"We've spent this whole time talking about me. I thought you had questions about work." She said wiping her mouth.

"I said I had questions; I never said they were work-related and you have answered them."

"You wanted to ask me personal questions. Why?" She said with a frown.

"Because I want to know you, the person."

"Why?"

Jackson smirked at Victoria's befuddlement. He leaned forward lowering his voice as if telling her a secret. "Honestly, because I'm curious by nature and I like you." He couldn't help, but to look into her eyes and then at her perfectly shaped lips as he said it. The way it came out sounded very intimate. He didn't mean for it to sound that way. She lowered her eyes from his. "I think you are a fascinating person Victoria." He added casually to ease her discomfort.

"Thank you." She said rising from the table to discard her

trash. Why on earth had he said he liked her and why did certain parts of her body react and start pulsing with its own heartbeat. It wasn't just that he said it, it was the way he looked at her mouth. It was intimate, and it was a little too intense for her.

He hadn't meant to say that he liked her, but it slipped out, and he couldn't take it back. He followed her to throw away his trash and held the door open for her. In the car, she asked what he thought of Laura and Jim. He told her that they both seemed confident and knowledgeable.

Jim was an older man who had years of sales experience and seemed interested in retiring to fish and golf all day. He talked about his family and how he was expecting his first grandson in a few months. Jackson liked him. He spent most of his meeting with Laura ignoring her flirtatious behavior. She was competent at her job but based on what she said about using all her assets; she used her sexuality to garner sales. He wasn't pleased with that. The product was exceptional, and she should be able to close deals based on the product and pricing.

When they arrived back at the office, she thanked him for lunch and told him she would send him some information via email about their product and programming so that he could get familiar with it before his meetings in the morning with the programmers. Then she sat at her desk answering customer emails.

As she put her purse in the drawer of her desk, her phone buzzed.
Sasha: "Did you have a nice lunch?"

She punctuated this with kissing emojis. Victoria quickly sent back a message expressing her feelings on the matter. She sent puking faces back along with one with its tongue stuck out.
Sasha giggled but did not send another message. Victoria

was grateful for that.

The rest of the afternoon went reasonably quickly, and Victoria and her team stayed busy with calls and email from customers. She had been so engrossed with work that she didn't realize that it was long past quitting time. It suddenly seemed very quiet in the office. She looked around and found that everyone had gone home. Someone from the programming and customer support teams stayed till eight each night to cover any emergency issues. They rotated days so that someone was available every night. Even they had left, and she was alone in the office.

She stretched her arms above her head rising from her chair. It was time to go home. Before leaving it might be smart to stop in the lady's room. When she finished in the stall and had washed her hands, she stood in front of the mirror. She had a slight headache. She rubbed her temples. Then she removed the pins holding the bun in place at the back of her head. She ran her fingers through her hair allowing the wavy length to flow past her shoulders. Her headache eased a bit.

Jackson looked at his watch; it was later than he thought. He had been studying the information Victoria had given him and time had gotten away from him. Jackson had also been handling Q.E. business via email through his cell phone. He got up from his desk to leave. He stopped when he saw Victoria standing in her workspace. She had her head down and her hair hung in waves around her. She raised her head, and their eyes met. "I thought everyone had gone. What are you still doing here?"

Victoria had thought the same thing. She assumed that she

was alone in the building. She had just pulled her keys out of her purse. "Working, what else? It came out with a bit of attitude.

Jackson moved towards her stopping only a few inches from her. "You don't like me. Don't try to deny it." He said looking down at her.

Victoria sighed. "I'm not very good at hiding my feelings." Jackson smiled in agreement. "It's not important what I think." She added looking away from him.

"It is to me. I'd like to know what is going on in there." He said pointing to her head.

Should she tell him? Maybe if she did, it would be like therapy for her, and she would be able just to accept that she had not gotten the job and she could move on. Go for it, she told herself. "After Angela left, Peter pretty much promised me your job. So, I'm a little pissed off about the fact that you're here." She said glancing up at him. "I work hard, and I feel like it's all for nothing sometimes and this seems to be a pattern in my life. It's not you."

He smiled softly at her confession. "I'm sorry. I had no idea." It wasn't him, the person, that she didn't like. It was that he had taken something she wanted.

She waved his apology away, "How could you know?" She grabbed her purse to leave.

"Have a drink with me?"

"I should get home." She said stepping around him.

"Please. It will make me feel better about stealing your job from you." He said grabbing her arm as she moved to pass him. "We could get to know each other and start over."

Victoria froze, the touch of his hand felt electric. A tingle ran down her spine. She knew she should say no and go home. "One drink."

# Chapter 4 One Drink

Jackson quickly realized that he could not go to any of the bars that he frequented for fear of being recognized. He tried to remember some out of the way place where he most likely would not run into anyone that he knew. As he locked up the office with the set of keys and security code Peter had given him Victoria stood quietly waiting for him to finish. It didn't take more than a few minutes to ensure that the office was secured. They discussed some options for where to go. "Shall we?" He asked once they had settled on a place not far from the office.

Victoria smiled and walked to her car. "I'll follow you. That way neither of us will have to come back to get our car." She slid into her car and followed Jackson as he led her to the Bryan Street Tavern, just east of downtown Dallas. Jackson parked and was standing beside her car as she got out.

They crossed the small parking lot and entered the tavern. When they arrived, Victoria paused to look around. There weren't many people inside. A few men sat at the bar, a couple sat at a table by the door, and a man was shooting pool in the back corner alone. The bartender smiled and said, "Welcome. Have a seat anywhere. I'll be right with you."

Jackson waved back. "Where would you like to sit, at the bar or a table?"

Victoria knew that the bar stools although padded was bound to be uncomfortable due to her large behind. "A table." She followed Jackson as he led her to the back near the pool table.

They sat, and the bartender appeared. "I'm Jasper. What

can I get you folks to drink?"

Jackson waited for Victoria to order. Victoria wasn't a drinker, so she had no idea what to order. "I'll have a long island iced tea." She said recalling the name of the drink from a time when she went out to dinner with Sasha and her husband. Victoria had a raspberry iced tea, but Sasha laughed at her and said that if she were going to have tea, she would have the Long Island iced tea. Jackson ordered a draft beer.

"The kitchen will be open for another hour. Just let me know if you want to order something to eat. Here are a couple of menus."

Jasper returned to the bar and proceeded to make their drinks. Victoria was busy checking the place out. There was lots of wood in this bar. The bar could easily seat ten people side by side. It was probably oak from its color. There were two large flat screen television sets mounted on the wall behind the bar. That wall was oak as well. The tables were all made of oak wood and even the floor. This establishment was definitely a man's domain. There weren't any mirrors hanging behind the bar no fancy art hung on the walls. There were some sports pictures and what looked like street signs hanging randomly around the room. There was a dartboard near the door and a jukebox near the hallway that undoubtedly led to the restrooms. She liked it all. It seemed like a genuine bar where regulars came in knew each other.

Jackson sat watching her look around the bar. He smiled. "What are you thinking?"

Victoria turned to him smiling. "I like it here." Jasper returned with their drinks.

Victoria sipped from the straw and loved the lovely taste of tea, sweetness, and alcohol. "I see why Sasha likes these," she said taking another sip.

"You've never had one before?"

"No." She said in between sips. "I'm not a drinker, but I like this," she said.

Jackson watched amused by her enthusiasm for the drink. He watched her licking her lips and became enthused himself. Jackson told himself that his agenda in asking her out was to gather more information about the people in the office. He knew he was lying to himself. "Do you and Sasha go out a lot?"

"Not lately. I think Sasha has finally gotten the message to stop trying to fix me up. She is so happy with her husband Brian that she wants everyone to fall in love." She stopped sipping her drink which was now half gone. She grabbed the menu looking over the selections. They apparently had a full kitchen. The menu offered several dishes and quite a few sides and desserts.

He had seen a picture that Sasha kept on her desk. He hadn't asked about it when he sat with her listening to calls. In the photo, Sasha was standing beside a tall African American man with two smiling girls in similar outfits standing in front of them. They looked like their father but had Sasha's Asian features. He watched Victoria as she flipped through the menu. "Would you like to order something?"

Victoria frowned. She did want to order something, but she had yet to make up for eating items off her diet twice this week. She laid the menu down and shook her head. "No." She changed the subject. "Do you go out a lot?

He used to go out a lot. He had always liked to party and have fun, but he spent so much time working to grow his business that he didn't have time for it now. "Not anymore. I'm too old for clubbing."

Victoria snorted in derision. "Too old? Please, try again."

"You don't think I'm too old for partying?" He asked drinking his beer.

"Um, no I don't. You're like what twelve or something, right?" Victoria joked sipping her drink.

Jackson chuckled, "I will have you know that I am thirty-two years old."

Victoria waved away the answer. "You're still a baby."

Jackson grinned at her. He liked this version of Victoria. Her eyes sparkled, and she was funny. "Babies can't drink beer." He said raising his glass to his mouth.

"Okay so you just graduated from breast milk," She teased.

He laughed at her comment. "I still like breast milk." He teased back, looking at her chest.

Victoria's face froze. This conversation was heading down the wrong road. He was flirting with her, and she could not fathom why? To change the subject, she asked him a question that had been plaguing her for a day or so. "How did you get this job. Peter didn't place an advertisement for it." She only knew this because in the past she had always been the one to place employment ads.

Jackson put his glass down. He never thought someone would ask this. "I met Peter through someone I know and mentioned I was looking for a new job." He lied to her. She seemed to be mulling it over. She sipped her drink and seemed disappointed when she realized it was gone. She waved to Jasper for another drink.

"You met him, and he just hired you like that?" She asked

snapping her fingers.

Jackson needed to get her mind off this subject. She was smart he knew that, and he couldn't take the chance of her picking apart his story. "It didn't happen quite as fast as that." Jasper set another drink in front of her and took her empty glass away. "Let's not talk about work."

"Alright what shall we talk about?"

An hour later Victoria realized she was working on her third drink and was feeling pretty good. Jackson had also continued to flirt with her off and on. They had been talking about being single and ended up talking about Sam and his tastes in men, when Jackson said, "What are your tastes in men?"

Victoria had replied, "I want what I can't have."

"What do you mean?" Jackson knew she was overly honest in part, because of the alcohol in her drink. He took advantage of her inebriated state, and he didn't feel sorry for it.

"You know what I'm saying. I'm curvy or whatever you want to call it, but I like men with tight toned bodies. You know the type of guy with abs for days, strong and muscular."

"Well, damn it all to hell," he said looking upset.

"What?" She asked curiously.

"I have abs for days." He raised his polo shirt showing her his well-defined abdomen. "I'm strong and have muscles," he said pumping up his biceps for her.

Boy did he have abs? She swallowed hard looking at the body underneath his shirt and his bulging bicep. He was exactly the physical type she liked. She felt the bubbles in her stomach again. "Excuse me." She pushed her chair away from the table. "I'll be right back."

Jackson watched as she moved past him slowly going down the hall before disappearing into the lady's room. She was attracted to him. He knew that. The way she looked at him as he displayed his attributes said it all.

Victoria used the facilities, and after washing her hands, she splashed water on her face. She was feeling hot suddenly. Three Long Island iced teas, Victoria had told him she would have one drink. She realized that she wouldn't be able to drive home. She'd have to Uber it tonight and have someone bring her to get her car tomorrow.

She returned to the table with her phone in her hand. "I need to get home." Before Jackson could protest that she shouldn't drive she continued, "I know I had too much to drink. Don't worry; Uber is on the way."

He would take her home, but he knew she would fight him on it. Jackson didn't want this to end, but he knew it had to at some point. He paid their bill and made sure that her car would be safe for the night. Jasper assured him that it would be okay. He even suggested that Jackson move it to the back of the bar, a more secure area with a gate that would be locked after closing. Jasper also let them know that he would be there after eight in the morning if they wanted to pick it up then.

Jackson left her inside while he moved her car. It was tiny, and he couldn't understand how she could feel comfortable driving it. It was more than five years old, and he noticed the high mileage on the odometer. She deserved to drive something better than this. He parked her car and made sure it was locked up before going back to Victoria.

They only had to wait a few minutes before her ride arrived. Jackson opened the back-passenger door for her. Before she could slide into the back seat, he slipped his arm around her waist and pulled her close to him. She tilted her head back about to ask what he was doing, but his lips touched hers, and she lost all thoughts. His kiss was soft but demanding, and it was incredibly intense for Victoria. When he pulled away from her, he looked into her eyes and said, "You can have what you want Victoria."

Just as easily as he had slid his arm around her waist, he removed it, and she got into the car. He closed the door watching as the car moved out of the parking lot and onto the street. Victoria Timmons was all he could think about on his way home.

# Chapter 5 No More Kisses

Jackson walked into the office just as Millie was hanging up the phone. "Vicky called, she said she's running late this morning. She said your info for the office contact sheet hadn't been added yet. You can email me with the best contact numbers to reach you, and I'll get it updated. I'll send you a copy."

"I'll do that right away." He said walking away from her. He had kicked himself mentally after he got in last night. He should have gotten her phone number so that he could make sure that she had made it home alright.

He had driven home thinking of how sweet the kiss was and how soft she felt as her flesh pressed against his. There was no denying that he had wanted her all night and her natural response to him made him think that she had wanted him too. She hadn't resisted his kiss, in fact, she seemed to melt into him.

An hour later Victoria knocked on his door. He was concentrating on the financial data that she had emailed him the day before. "Do you have a moment?"

"Sure." He said smiling brightly at her. She had her hair pulled back in a bun again. She was wearing gray slacks and a red button down short sleeved shirt. She did look good in red. She came in closing the door behind her.

"This is about last night," she said coming to his desk. She stopped but didn't sit down. "I had too much to drink." She paused weighing her words. "Not that I'm using that as an excuse, but what happened between us, can never happen again."

Jackson frowned. "You mean me kissing you?" he asked rising from his chair moving around the desk. He stopped so close to her that Victoria had to take a step back to look into his eyes.

"Yes. No more kisses." Victoria shook her head when she said it.

"I liked kissing you." He said with a smirk. Her heart rate sped up. "Didn't you like kissing me?"

Victoria swallowed, "No."

"No?" he asked pulling her close. He flicked his tongue over her lips, and when she responded with a sigh, he captured her lips in a kiss that made her moan with desire. She wanted to push him away as her hands moved to his chest, but the feel of his hard-muscular body made her step closer molding her body to his. She opened her mouth to him as he explored her sweet mouth with his tongue. His hands moved to cup her ass. He squeezed it. He loved the softness. She moaned again, a sound that he could easily get used to hearing. He wanted to continue this exploration of her soft curvy body but now was not the right time or place. He reluctantly pulled his mouth from hers and met her eyes, smiling. "Liar."

Victoria was breathing heavily as she tried to understand what just happened. She didn't know what to say. She only knew that this had to stop. There were so many reasons why this was wrong.

She took a step back and then another. Once she felt safe, she said, "We can't do this."

"Why not?"

"First, you are my boss. That's inappropriate. Second, I'm too old for you. Third..." She couldn't think of a third reason.

Jackson smiled, "First, there is nothing in the employee handbook that says we can't date as long as it's consensual. Second, I like antiques." He shrugged his shoulders as he grinned at the last part, hoping to lighten the mood.

"Asshole," she smiled as she said it.

"So, there is a slight age difference between us, but the differences are what makes this so much fun."

As he moved closer to her Victoria took another step back. "Stop right there."

He stopped. "One date. One real date. We will go out to dinner and a movie or something. We will do whatever you want to do. If, after that date, if you still want to deny that you want me, I will leave you alone." He had no intention of doing so, but he wasn't going to tell her that.

Victoria didn't know why she was considering this at all, but she was. "I don't think..." She started to say something.

"Don't think," he interrupted. "Just say yes." He had already figured out that Victoria was an analyzer of all things. She did it in her job. It came naturally to her to pick everything apart until she understood it, until it made sense to her.

Victoria sighed. "Yes." Before she knew it, he had crossed the space between them and had her in his arms. This time she did push at his chest. "No more kisses in the office," she said trying to get out of his grasp.

He latched on to the end of her statement, 'in the office.' He fully intended to kiss her a lot when they weren't in the office. "Deal." He said letting her go and extending his hand for her to shake. Victoria shook his hand and returned to her desk.

She sat down thinking, what have I done? She tried not to

think about it too much. She had only known him for a few days, and he was her boss, but wow, the man could kiss. Every time his lips touched hers, she felt like her mind had shut down. That was the problem. Her brain had taken a vacation. She shook it off and got back to work.

Sasha: "How late did you work last night? Sam said you were still here when he left."

Victoria: "Not too long after that."

Sasha: "He said Mr. Hottie was still here too."

Victoria: "Who?"

Sasha stood and came around to Victoria's side of the cubicle wall. "You know who," she said pointing to Jackson's office.

Victoria smiled without looking up. "Yes, he was still here. I didn't know it until I was on my way out." Victoria quickly realized that Sasha was not going away without asking or saying something that she thought was important. Victoria turned away from the customer email she was reading. "You have my full attention."

Sasha smiled. "You know Millie watches the feed from the security cameras every morning."

Victoria did not know that. "She does? Why?"

"Peter asked her to a while back. He thought someone was lurking around outside or something. It turns out it was nothing, but she still watches it every day. She says she has seen some interesting things on it. She watches the tape at high speed unless she sees something that she wants to see in detail. Guess what she saw on the video from last night."

"I don't know." Victoria lied. She knew precisely what Millie had seen, Jackson and her leaving the building together, but that's all it was.

"She saw you waiting for the hottie to lock up and then the two of you having a chat."

Victoria shrugged her shoulders, "Okay. Is that all?"

Sasha looked frustrated. Victoria knew that she was expecting some juicy account of their conversation, which she was not going to provide. "What were you talking about?"

"Sasha, for real? If you must know, he was asking for directions." Victoria wasn't lying, but she was stretching the truth.

"Damn," Sasha said disappointed with the answer. "I just knew he was hitting on you. I still think he likes you."

Victoria smiled at Sasha. "You know what I think? I think you need to get back to work and stop gossiping."

Sasha laughed and went back to her side of the cubicle. She peeked over the wall. "I know attraction when I see it, and it's not gossip until I say it behind your back."

Victoria laughed and went back to her work. She was going to have to keep this date with Jackson under wraps. If Sasha got wind of it, she'd be planning their wedding and baby showers. Sasha told Victoria repeatedly, that she was way too awesome to be single and that there was a man out there made just for her.

She had agreed to go out with him, but in her mind, that was all that would happen. One date and she would let him know that it was not going beyond that. Men complicated everything. She was trying to achieve business success and take care of her aging mother. She didn't have time for a man.

Jackson knew that Victoria was probably at her desk plotting a way out of the date. He had no intention of allowing her to. He needed to cement their deal immediately and get her to commit to a specific day and time. He opened the office messenger and typed, "Is Friday or Saturday better for you?" He waited for her reply.

A few seconds later his cell phone indicated that he had a new text from Victoria's number. He had programmed it in after Millie sent him the updated contact list.

Victoria: "Never on the office IM. It's monitored."

She hadn't answered his question. He sent a message to her phone.

Jackson: "Friday or Saturday?"

He sat staring at his phone.

Victoria: "Neither, I'm busy. I think we should forget the whole thing."

She wasn't getting out of this.

Jackson: "No way, we made a deal. Pick a day or else!"

Victoria stared at her phone. What did he mean or else?

Victoria: "Or else what?"

She waited and then the text appeared.

Jackson: "Or else I will come out there and kiss you in front of the whole office."

He wouldn't dare? After thinking about it, she knew that he

probably would. She wanted to keep this thing between them.

Jackson waited and was about to get up and prove his point when his text alert sounded.

Victoria: "I can't go this weekend. How about lunch on Monday?"

Victoria's leg shook nervously as she waited.

Jackson: "Rejected, lunch is not a real date, and you know it. I will accept Monday evening. Send me your address. I'll pick you up at seven."

Victoria: "I will meet you, just tell me where."

Victoria sent back to him. She didn't need him coming to her house.

Jackson: "No deal. When I date a woman, I treat her like a lady. I open doors, pull out chairs and I pick them up for dates."

A lady in the streets and a freak in the sheets, she bet. Reluctantly she sent him her address.

# Chapter 6 The Date/Cooking with Caroline

Jackson sat in Peter's office quietly listening as Peter talked. Jackson knew that he should be paying more attention to what Peter was saying, but his mind was on Victoria. She had agreed to go on a date with him, and Jackson wanted to make sure it was perfect. He knew that she was determined not to get involved with him. She had stated her ideas clearly, but he intended to prove to her that her reasons weren't applicable.

Peter was staring at him. Jackson had missed something important he gathered. "I'm sorry, can you say that last part again?"

"I want to know what your thoughts are so far. I know that this is just a business deal for you, but you've been here a few days."

Jackson pushed thoughts of Victoria out of his head and focused on Peter and his purpose for being in this building. "I am still meeting with the staff, but I can already see that you have some people that I could use."

"Good," Peter said sighing heavily. He was concerned about Victoria more than most. She was dedicated and hardworking and carried the burden of caring for her mother. There were others that he knew needed their jobs just as much, but they were far younger and some married, so they had some support structure to help them stay afloat.

Jackson listened for more than an hour as Peter gave him recommendations regarding the strengths and weaknesses of the people he had been working and talking to over the past few days. Peter pointed out their achievements and accomplishments as well as telling him areas that he thought they could improve.

Jackson agreed with most of his observations. Peter leaned back in his chair and asked, "What are your thoughts on Victoria?"

"I think that she has enormous potential. She is smart, intuitive, and hard working. She has the potential to go far in business with the right guidance." Jackson noticed that Peter seemed to relax a bit at what he said. Victoria was one of the people he wanted to ensure wasn't decimated by their deal.

Jackson returned to his office to find Victoria near the office supplies. She had her back to him. He took a second to enjoy the view. She had her hair pulled back as usual. Today she was wearing a top that exposed the lovely brown skin of her shoulders. It was soft looking and loose fitting. Victoria was wearing pants again. She looked great in them, but he preferred to see her legs. He would have to see if he could entice her to wear more dresses and skirts as well as heels.

She turned and caught him staring at her. "How was your meeting with Peter?"

Jackson answered moving towards his desk. "It went well." He lowered his voice, "You look lovely today."

Victoria turned to make sure no one was close by and then glared at Jackson.

He chuckled, "What, I can't pay you a compliment?"

"No. Now stop distracting me. I'm doing inventory, so I can order supplies." She turned her back to him, which in his opinion was as lovely a view as the front.

Victoria finished her inventory and returned to her desk to place the order. Peter buzzed her phone asking her to come to his office. She hadn't talked to him much this week. He usually came out to speak to her regarding various things, but this week he had confined himself to his office for the most part. She let Sasha and Sam know where she was going and walked down the hall.

The door was open. "Come in and close the door." She did as he asked and then sat in the chair across from his desk. "How are things going with Jackson?"

"Okay, I guess. Jackson's getting familiar with how we do things and he's made some suggestions for improvements."

"Is he getting along with everyone?"

"Sure." She said, not quite sure what he was expecting her to say. "He has sat with Sam and Sasha while they worked. He's sitting in with the programmers and tech guys this afternoon."

"What's your impression of him," Peter asked her, leaning forward with interest in her response.

I think he's trouble with a capital T, she thought. That was because he was causing havoc with her body ever since he kissed her, but she knew Peter meant in the business sense. "I think he will be good for Albrecht Armor. He is taking the concerns and issues we need to deal with seriously, but only time will tell. You wouldn't have hired him if he couldn't handle the job, so I'm trusting him as you asked me too."

"Good." He said relaxing back in the chair.

Victoria wished Peter would tell her what was going on. He wasn't behaving like himself, and she knew it had something to do with Jackson. Peter didn't ask any more questions about Jackson. He did ask about her mother and if she was enjoying the new house. She told him her mother was doing well and that she was enjoying her new home.

She told him about some of the work that she had planned, like the new privacy fence and the yard work she planned to do herself. The property had no trees when she bought it, and she intended to plant a tree in the front and back yards. She also wanted to add a rose bush near the living room entrance. Those things were down the road a bit.

Victoria's weekend went quickly. She worked her part-time hustle Friday night until midnight and then all-day Saturday and Sunday. She was exhausted by the time Monday morning dawned. If she had gotten the promotion and raise, she would have been able to take the weekends for herself. She would be able to spend time with her mother doing fun things maybe even pursue a hobby, but that, unfortunately, didn't happen and to meet her ever-growing expenses she had to work two jobs.

Jackson hadn't tried to kiss her again in the office, but he did send subtle messages every time they were alone, even if it were only for a few moments. He looked at her mouth regularly as she spoke to him. Jackson would sometimes stand extremely close to her. He sent lewd text messages to her phone throughout the day. She should be offended, but she wasn't. She found herself more aroused by the second. She had also begun to feel anxious waiting to see what he might send next.

It had started on Thursday night after she left work.

Jackson "I can't wait to kiss you."

She hadn't responded to it.

Jackson: "Your lips are so soft and sweet."

She didn't respond to that one either. Then Jackson sent the kissing emoji, which made her giggle.

Victoria: "You are silly. Don't you have something better to do than text me all night."

Jackson: "There are a few things I'd like to do that would be better than texting, and they all involve you."

Victoria could only imagine what things he might mean. She chose not to respond. On Saturday and Sunday while she was working his messages started.

Jackson: "Good morning beautiful."

Most of the day he sent texts.

Jackson: "Thinking of you.
Jackson: "Hope you're having a good day.
Jackson: "I can't wait until Monday."

All which Victoria thought was sweet. Each time her text alert went off, and it wasn't one of her customers she smiled a little bit brighter.

Jackson ran his hand through his hair. He couldn't believe what he had just heard Hank say. "I'll come out to the house after work, and we'll figure this out." He disconnected the call.

His father had been caught leaving a hotel with a woman other than his mother by a photographer who had just sold the pictures to a media outlet. The woman who handled his mother's public relations had been contacted. They wanted to interview his mother regarding the indiscretion.

She was a public figure serving on many boards of charities, and as a public figure, her life was going to be scrutinized. This was also not good for Quinn Enterprises. The negative publicity would cost them some stock points over the next weeks until this died down.

When he called his mother on Friday, she had been crying. She tried to hide it, but Jackson could hear it in her voice. His father had cheated before, but his mother always forgave her husband, and they would be happy until Doug did it again. He didn't understand why she put up with his callous behavior.

"Dad, we have to get around this now. Who is she? Maybe we can offer her something to keep her quiet and make her go away," Beth said. She didn't want to keep handing out their money like offering tic-tacs to someone with bad breath, but they needed this to die down quickly so that when they announced the acquisition of Albrecht Armor their stock wouldn't be rebounding but in a stable position.

"There is nothing to get around," Doug said pouring a brandy.

"There's nothing to get around because his whore is quite happy with her apartment, car and lavish lifestyle." His mother who had been sitting quietly by the fireplace finally spoke. "This one has been smarter than the others apparently." Jackson watched as his mother stood from her position on the sofa in the drawing room, walked to his father and slapped his face before leaving the room.

His father left the room as well heading in the opposite direction from his mother. Jackson was tired of this. For many years his father had tried to keep his women a secret, but lately, he didn't seem to care who knew. Jackson had tried to convince his mother to divorce him, but she refused, and he didn't understand why.

His sister felt pretty much the way he did about their father's cheating. Jackson later told Hank to find out who this woman was. He wasn't going to leave this to his father to handle. It was clear that his father wasn't capable of handling anything.

The three of them talked about how things were going at Albrecht. He told them that he was pleasantly surprised by some of the employees and how this acquisition could serve them in multiple ways. A couple of the tech guys would be great for their gaming division.

He spent some time with his grandfather. Grandpa Jack wanted to know when he was getting married. He wasn't happy when he told him that it might be a while. He wanted great-grandchildren, and he kept saying that he'd probably die before either of his grandchildren provided any.

Victoria looked at the clock; it was almost three. She had been busy all day, but she had gotten caught up on nearly all her work. Jackson was a quick learner and had taken over several of the duties that she had been doing since Angela left the company. It was so slow that Sasha and Sam were chatting while waiting for the phones to ring. Jackson stepped out of his office and came to the group of cubicles where they sat. "It seems really slow today. Victoria, why don't you take the rest of the afternoon off."

Victoria looked at him curiously and then to Sasha and Sam. Sasha raised one eyebrow, pursing her lips.

Victoria was tired, and she could use a nap. "Thanks Jackson." She said pulling her purse from under her desk. Jackson went back into his office. Sasha leaned over the desk. "I'm telling you he likes you. He didn't tell Sam or me to go home."

"Bye Sasha," Victoria said smiling and standing up. "Don't be jealous that I'm leaving early for a change."

As Victoria got to her car, her phone chirped.

Jackson: "Take a nap, have a bubble bath. I want you well rested for tonight, and by the way, the attire is sexy casual."

Sexy casual? He had punctuated this with the flirty emoji. Did she look that tired? What on earth was he planning for their date? She hoped he didn't think he was going to get any.

Jackson could see that Victoria was tired. He wanted this date to go well. Jackson knew that if it didn't, she would hold him to their deal. He wanted more than one date with her, and he was going to do everything he could to ensure that they had a great time tonight and to make sure she could not deny her attraction to him.

Tonight, Sam was on the schedule to stay to cover the support calls and emails. He didn't want it to look too obvious that he favored Victoria, an hour later he let Sasha go home as well. He did the same thing with the tech guys.

He had just finished his shower and was contemplating shaving his five o'clock shadow when his phone rang. He checked the caller ID fearing that Victoria was calling to cancel. He sighed with relief when he saw Hank's name. "Hey, buddy." He said answering the call.

"Hey, I was checking in to see how things are going over at Albrecht. Maybe we can grab a drink tonight and talk about it."

"No can do. I have plans tonight."

Hank snorted into the phone. "What kind of plans? Can't you

push it back and have one drink?"

"I've got a date, and it wasn't easy to get it, so no I can't push it back." He didn't want to tell Hank who he was taking out. Hank might recognize Victoria's name since he was involved with the deal with the company.

"Difficult for you to get a date? I like her already. Well alright. We need to get together this week." Hank said as he mentioned some business deals that they needed to discuss.

After his call with Hank, he decided not to shave. He wanted to look a little less like the persona he had created and more like himself. He styled his hair a little neater than the bed head style he'd been sporting. Instead of a polo or boring plaid shirt, he put on a clean, crisp white button-down tucking it in his dark blue denim jeans. He did wear the glasses, and while he looked like himself, he still looked like the character he was portraying. He splashed on some cologne and slipped his feet into black loafers, and he was ready.

Victoria stood looking at herself in the mirror. She wasn't sure if what she had chosen to wear would be considered sexy casual. Victoria wanted to put on a pair of sweatpants and t-shirt. The dress she picked was a soft denim material, cut asymmetrically. It stopped above her knees in the front and hung to mid-calf in the back. She had rolled up the long sleeves so that they stayed at her elbows. It was casual for sure. She rarely wore heels, but she chose a pair of tan, peep toe, platform sandals and a matching tan clutch.

The doorbell rang. Victoria turned to make sure she looked okay from the back. Her mother was in her room in the back of the house, and Victoria knew she wouldn't hear the ringing sound. She had already told her mother she was going out but didn't disclose with who. She opened the door to find a very sexy Jackson waiting for her.

"Wow." He said smiling. "You look incredible."

"Thank you." She said blushing at his compliment.

"You ready?" He asked still smiling at her. She was gorgeous. She was wearing her hair on top of her head in a sexy, messy ball with curly tendrils hanging temptingly around her face and neck. Victoria had beautiful brown skin and from what he could tell she was only wearing lip gloss and mascara.

"Let me just tell my mother I'm leaving. I'll be right out."

Jackson waited on the porch as she left him and disappeared through a door off the living room. A few seconds later she was back. She closed and locked the door. Once they were in the car, she asked, "Where are we going?"

"I was having a hard time coming up with something for us to do tonight. I didn't want this to be just a boring dinner date. I had to get creative." He said still not telling her where they were going.

"That doesn't answer my question." She said smiling at him. She was trying not to be excited about spending time with him.

"I know, I want it to be a surprise. I think this is going to be fun and memorable." He said winking at her.

Victoria didn't have much choice but to go along with him. It took about twenty minutes to get to their destination. Where ever he was taking her was in the up and coming Trinity Groves area of Dallas. He pulled into a strip of businesses, mostly restaurants and found a parking space. Victoria had been here a few times picking up food for her customers. He parked and came around to open her door and to help her out of the car. He held her hand as they walked toward a row of restaurants. She had never been the hand holding, public display of affection type, but Victoria liked the feel of his hand in hers.

He led her to a place called Sinful Cooking with Caroline. As they entered, she noted that it wasn't a restaurant. There were tables set for two in the front, as well as a bar with about ten bar stools. There was a counter with display cases of items for sale and a young lady behind the register. Near a hallway leading further into the establishment, there was a chalkboard sign that read, Couples cooking class this way. Jackson had signed them up for a couple's cooking class. As he pushed through the swinging door at the end of the hallway, he turned his face to her, smiling.

She was amazed. She would never have thought to do this on a date. They were greeted by a lively young lady with auburn hair wearing an apron that said I'm Caroline.

"Hello, I'm Caroline." She shook their hands as Jackson introduced them.

"I'm Jackson, and this is Victoria."

"Welcome. We have one more couple coming tonight. Why don't you two have a seat at the table, and we'll get started as soon as everyone is here." She indicated a large round table with chairs all around it. Three other couples were sitting there chatting.

Just as they got comfortable in their seats the last couple arrived. Once they were seated, Caroline spoke to the group. "Welcome everyone. As I said I'm Caroline, I'm glad you all could make it to my cooking for couples' class. Before I tell you what fun we will have tonight, let's all introduce ourselves to one another and tell us why you're here tonight. Why don't you two start." She said pointing to a man and woman near her.

They introduced themselves and stated their reasons for being there. Most of the couples said they were there to try something fun and different together. When it was their turn, Jackson spoke. "I'm Jackson, and this is Victoria. This is our first date. It took a lot of convincing to get her to go out with me, and I wanted it to be something she would never forget or regret." The women in the group all smiled and awed at them.

When everyone had taken their turn, Caroline outlined their evening. "Tonight, is not about how well you cook or how the food comes out. That being said, you all will be eating what you cook tonight. It's about working as a team. You and your significant other will have your own kitchen station to work in. There is a card in each location with a dish type that you are to make. By the time everyone is done, we will have all the components of a whole meal including dessert. There are cookbooks in each station if you need them. Every ingredient you will need is at your station, if not let me know. All the stations are set up the same, so it doesn't matter which one you choose. You have one hour to prepare your dish. There are warming trays in each station. If you finish quickly, you can pop your items into the warmer and help your fellow group members with their dishes if you like.

Once the meal is complete, it will be set up buffet style, and you will serve yourselves. As you can see," Caroline pointed behind them, "we have set up intimate tables for two, where you will have a romantic dinner with your partner. At the end of the meal, guess who does the cleanup? You do as a team. Are we ready?" she asked them. They all responded positively and moved to select their workspace.

Jackson followed Victoria as she decided which station they would work in. She looked at the card laying on their station. "Looks like we get to make the dessert." She said showing him the card. He watched as she found a place out of the way to stash her purse.

"What should we make?" He asked leaning his hips on the counter and folding his arms over his chest. "I'm leaving it up to you. I am no good in the kitchen."

Victoria saw the cookbook laying near the sink and went to look through it. "Let's see what we can come up with." She said flipping through the dessert section. Jackson moved to stand behind her. He was close enough for her to feel his body heat.

"A cake maybe?" He suggested resting his chin on her shoulder. He was trying not to touch her, but she was very enticing.

"Maybe." She said still flipping pages. He was too close to her for her comfort. She closed the book and moved away from him. "Cake may be too heavy. Since we don't know what the others are going to cook, we should do something light and fun."

Jackson stood watching her. He could see the wheels turning as she came up with an idea. She stood there making a steeple with her fingers. She bit her lip and closed her eyes in concentration. It took every ounce of strength he had not to kiss her silly. Then she opened her eyes and smiled at him.

"I've got it. There's not a name for this, at least not that I know of. It's just something I make when I want a sweet snack, and I'm trying not to have something fattening or heavy, and it takes no time to make. It's kind of like nacho chips, but sweet." She turned and started opening cabinets and drawers pulling out items and putting them on the counter.

While she did that, Jackson grabbed the aprons sitting on the counter. He put one on himself. Jackson waited until

Victoria turned to face him and slipped the top over her head, quickly reaching around her to tie it in the back. He caught her by surprise.

Victoria was engrossed in finding what they would need she didn't realize that he was standing behind her. She allowed him to put the apron on her. His hand grazed her bottom, and Victoria remembered the way his hand felt when he had kissed her in his office. She raised her head to look into his eyes. He smiled and kissed the tip of her nose. "Now, you won't ruin your clothes. She was blushing. Her face felt warm.

"Thank you." She said moving around him to the oven. She set the temperature.

"What can I do?"

She looked to where she had some things laid out, then to him. "We need baking trays, three or four should do, parchment paper, and see if you can find cookie cutters."

Jackson chuckled, "Okay I know what baking trays are and cookie cutters, but parchment paper, I have no clue about."

"I will get that." She said winking at him.

When they had all the things they needed, she and Jackson washed their hands and measured out their ingredients to begin mixing them. Jackson followed her directions and asked questions about why she was using certain things. She answered readily, and he learned that she liked to cook. They were making dough from flour, lard, a pinch of salt, baking powder, and warm water. She told him that what she was using could be made to make tortillas if you cooked them in a pan on the stove top, but that they were going to bake them in the oven with cinnamon and sugar. "We are making chips that we are going to drizzle with chocolate."

He watched as she poured the water into the mixing bowl and the dry ingredients become doughy. When the texture was right she stopped the mixture. "Will you get the cutting board and rolling pin please?"

Jackson found the items where she had the rest of the things she had assembled and brought them to her. "What now?" He asked watching her as she sprinkled the board with flour.

"Now you get your hands dirty." She giggled as she broke off a piece of the dough and rolled it into a ball with her hands. She instructed him to rub some flour on the rolling pin and then to sprinkle some on the dough ball she had placed on the board. Jackson did as she told him. She smiled her approval. "Now you are going to use the rolling pin to roll out the dough."

She watched as he grabbed the rolling pin and rolled the pin over the dough. She reached over putting her hands on top of his. "Like this, with just a bit of pressure." Even covered with flour, he loved the way her hands felt against his skin. She let go and continued making balls out of the dough, placing them into a glass bowl that she threw a dish towel over. "Flip it over and roll from the other side as well." I'll get the pans ready."

As all the couples were working, Caroline walked into their stations talking to them. As Victoria was melting butter in a bowl in the microwave Caroline stood watching Jackson. "What are you two making?"

Without hesitation, Jackson said, "We are making Tory's sweet Nachos."

"Sounds interesting." She asked Jackson a few more questions before moving on.

Once he had the dough thin as she had instructed, she took the melted butter and a teaspoon of vanilla and mixed them together. She brushed some onto the parchment paper she had used to line the pans. Then she asked him for the cookie cutters. "Cute." She said smiling as he handed her the cookie cutter shaped like a heart."

"It's supposed to be romantic, right?"

"Yes." He watched as she pressed the cookie cutter into the dough, turning it this way and that to get most of the dough used. Then she started placing them on the baking sheets, again turning them this way and that to fit as many as she could onto the pan. When she had used all the heart shapes, she took the leftover dough and made a new ball of it. "Now we will brush these with the butter, vanilla mix. You can start rolling out more dough." While he did his job, she brushed on the mixture and then sprinkled the mix of cinnamon and sugar over the heart-shaped dough.

She moved the pan to the side and helped him roll out another ball of dough. Once they had two pans of heart-shaped chips ready, she placed them in the oven and set the timer. While they worked, Jackson asked her typical first date questions. He started with asking if she had lived here her whole life. She explained that she had been born in Colorado and her family moved here to be closer to her mother's family. Her father traveled a lot and wanted his girls to be close to family. Her mother was legally blind, and because of her limited sight, he wanted them to have as much support as they could when he was out on the road. He had been a truck driver hauling loads all over the country.

Victoria was very animated as she talked about her mother and father and how happy her childhood had been. The only time he sensed any sadness at all was when she told him that her father had died just before her sixteenth birthday. She shook it off, and while Jackson finished up the last batch for the oven she began washing dishes in the sink. When the first round of heart-shaped chips was ready to come out of the oven, she was finishing the last few items, so he grabbed the oven mitt and pulled the pans from the oven and then placed the next two pans in and reset the timer.

Their next task, while the chips cooled was to make the chocolate sauce for the drizzle. Jackson helped by following her instructions. She told him how much sugar, and cocoa powder to measure out and put into the clean glass bowl. Victoria showed him how to whisk them together to remove lumps. She moved over to the stove and heated up milk, butter and vanilla extract in a saucepan. When the butter melted, Victoria whisked the dry ingredients into the milk mixture a little at a time. She took a serving spoon and showed him how to drizzle the chocolate over the chips in a zig-zag pattern.

Once the chocolate had cooled using a spatula she arranged the chips on five plates with small bowls of the still warm chocolate in the center of the dishes. It looked delicious, and Jackson couldn't wait to try one. He tried to snatch one while she turned her back but got caught before he could get his hands on one, she laughed as she looked over her shoulder, "Don't you dare touch that."

"Fine." He said standing beside her bumping her hip with his. "Good things come to those who wait." He took the dishes and utensils that were clean and started drying them. This was nice.

# Chapter 7 The Date/The Best Kiss

After dinner and the cleanup, Jackson held her hand as they walked back to the car. She stopped at the car door to allow him to open it. When he didn't pull the handle, she turned to look at him. He smiled at her and said, "We're not in the office." Before it registered what he meant, he cupped her face with his hands and kissed her slowly and deliberately.

His lips were soft as he brushed them over hers, once then again before sucking on them individually. Victoria sighed relaxing as her hand found its way up his chest. Jackson pressed her back against the car as one hand traveled down to her waist. He squeezed the soft flesh of her breast briefly, rubbing his thumb over the material covering her nipple as his hand moved lower. He liked that they were luscious, and her nipples grew hard as he touched her. Victoria moaned as her other hand grabbed the back of his neck.

She hadn't been kissed or touched in this way for a while. Jackson moved his other hand to her waist and ground himself against her, leaving no doubt that he wanted her. Victoria felt the slickness between her thighs and thought, if his kisses are this good, I can't wait to see what the dick is like. He pulled his mouth from hers, trailing his tongue along her jaw and down the side of her neck, stopping only to ask, "Did you have fun tonight?"

"Yes," she said when he continued his exploration.

"Will you go out with me again?" Victoria didn't answer right away. She knew she was supposed to be resisting his charms. She didn't see how this could be anything but a brief affair and when it was over, she would have to face him every day at work.

Jackson growled when she didn't respond and nipped at her earlobe as he rubbed his hardness against her. "You want me, say yes."

She tried to resist, she did. Somewhere between the flashes of heat, he was causing in her body; she gave in. "Yes."

"Yes, what?" He wanted to hear her say it.

"Yes, I want you, and yes I'll go out with you again. Yes, damn it." She forced out pushing her hands against his chest. He smiled and placed one last kiss on her lips before opening the car door for her.

On the ride back to Victoria's house, Jackson held her hand, playfully kissing the back of it occasionally. They didn't talk much. Victoria was second-guessing herself about her decision. She was thinking negatively, and she knew it, but she found it harder and harder to resist his charm. As he turned into her driveway, she pulled her hand from his and said, "We have to have some ground rules if we are going to see each other."

Jackson stopped the car and got out to open her door. "Okay, what kind of rules are we talking about?" He followed her to the door.

Victoria unlocked the door and turned off the alarm. "Come in." She said flipping the light switch next to the door. "I'll be right back. I just need to let my mother know I'm home."

Jackson stood in Victoria's living room taking it in. It was cozy with a long sofa and a chair facing a large flat screen television. He moved around looking at the photos hanging on the walls in various places. There were pictures of what he assumed were her parents and grandparents judging by the style of the clothing. Some were of Victoria at different ages. She was always smiling brightly.

Victoria found her mother in bed already, but not asleep. "Momma, I'm back."

"Did you have a good time baby?" Her mother asked from under the covers.

"Yes, we are going to sit in the living room for a little while and chat. I just wanted you to know I was home."

"Okay," Helen said yawning, Victoria kissed her cheek and left the room. "Goodnight."

When she returned to the living room, she found Jackson sitting on the couch looking delicious and comfortable with his thighs slightly spread apart, one arm on the armrest and the other along the back. She wanted to sit next to him, but she knew that was asking for trouble. She sat in the chair which swiveled and turned to face him. "I would have introduced you to her, but she's in bed already."

Jackson was amused by Victoria's need to sit in the chair instead of next to him. "No problem. I'm sure I will get to meet her soon. Now let's talk about these rules. We already have the no kissing at work rule."

He was making fun of her. "I don't want everyone in the office knowing my business that's all. There is to be no fraternization on company grounds or at any time when we are around people from the office."

"Okay, I can accept that. What else?" He said leaning his elbows on his knees with his hands together watching her intently.

"I can only go out Monday, Tuesday or Wednesday nights."

"Unacceptable. I will not be forced to wait for days between kisses." He said sitting back. "The longest I will go is forty-eight hours, and that is pushing it." He grinned as he said the last part.

Victoria needed to work her hustle on Saturday and Sunday. She could earn up to three hundred dollars easy on those days. "Alright and Friday night."

"Any other rules?"

Victoria couldn't think of any now, but she wanted the option to add rules when necessary. "For now, no. I reserve the right to add to and or amend slash change these rules at any time."

Jackson grinned at her, "As long as I'm allowed to negotiate for fairness I have no problem with that."

"You've got yourself a deal." She watched as Jackson leaned forward and slid down onto the floor moving towards her like a jungle cat stalking his prey. "What are you doing?"

"Sealing the deal with a kiss," he said as he reached her. He stopped in front of her rising on his knees. They were almost face to face. He grabbed her hips and pulled her forward, spreading her legs so that he was nestled between her thighs. He took her mouth, thrusting his tongue between her lips. Involuntarily her arms went around his shoulders as she kissed him back. His hands roamed up her back pressing her closer to his chest. He tore his lips from hers and kissed her chin before burying his face in her throat and chest. She smelled beautiful, feminine and floral.

Victoria felt his hands move around to the front of her undoing the buttons of her dress. "We can't, My mother..."

"I'm only going to kiss you, I promise." He said looking into her eyes before kissing each breast through the lacy material covering them. He ran his fingers along the edge of her bra before pulling the fabric down so that he could continue his exploration with his tongue. Jackson smiled wickedly as Victoria squirmed when he cupped her breasts in his hands pushing them together, kissing and sucking on each puckered bit of skin.

He pulled back and finished undoing the buttons of her dress. Pushing the material aside, he kissed her stomach, swirled his tongue around her belly button and then ran his tongue across the top of her lacy panties. She sighed, laying her head back on the chair. Jackson took advantage of her resignation. He slid his hand between the denim dress and the lace. Grabbing hold of them, Jackson lifted her up and slid them over her wonderfully soft behind and down her thighs. Once he had pushed them past her ankles and helped her step out of them, he looked into her eyes, placing his finger on his lips, "Shush. It's just a kiss."

Jackson pushed her legs up and out, spreading them over the arms of the chair. Victoria whimpered as he placed feather light kisses up and down her thighs. Jackson rubbed his stubble over her thighs while kissing her. He ran his thumb from the top of her opening to the bottom, loving how wet she was. When his thumb was coated with her juices, he opened her nether lips and applied light pressure rubbing circles.

Victoria's thighs quivered, and she bit her lip to keep quiet. She felt tortured, in the most delightful way. When he latched on to her love nub and began to suck and lick it passionately, she moaned profoundly squeezing her legs together. Jackson splay his hands on her thighs holding them apart as he quickened his actions. She could feel her orgasm building, and it didn't take long to get there. It had been a long time, and she was more than ready to cum for him.

Jackson loved the taste of her, the sounds she was trying so hard not to make as he inserted his finger into her and found her g-spot. He applied pressure causing her to moan louder.

Jackson continued to have his way, but he didn't want her mother to walk in on them. He removed his other hand from her thigh and used it to cover her mouth as she exploded in his mouth and all over his hand.

Victoria didn't mind his covering her mouth as she came. She had never had an orgasm that intense. Jackson kept his finger inside her as he rose to kiss her and suddenly Victoria was having another orgasm, and it was more intense than the first. Her eyes watered and she groaned and moaned into his mouth. She grabbed his wrist, trying to push him away as he continued to finger her to another sinful explosion.

Jackson slowly slid his finger from her but continued to kiss her until she slumped in the chair and grew quiet. She opened her eyes looking at him, and the smug bastard grinned from ear to ear, sucked the finger he had just extracted from her and said, "I like kissing you."

Victoria was blushing, and it was the most endearing thing he had ever seen. He picked up her panties and slid them into his front jeans pocket before standing. He scooped her up and set her on her feet buttoning her dress after fixing her bra. "I should go."

Her legs were wobbly as she followed him to the door. He kissed her sweetly one last time before leaving. Victoria closed the door, locked it and leaned her head against it, thinking that was the best kiss she ever had.

Jackson drove home happier and hornier than he had felt in a long time. He had wanted to do much more with Victoria, but he also wanted to savor every moment. He intended to take his time, and he didn't want her to have to be quiet.

He reflected on their conversation over dinner. They had shared food with each other and a lot of their history. Victoria asked him to tell her about his childhood. He told her the truth for the most part. Jackson said to her that he was born in Plano and had lived in the area all his life, that he had one sibling, a sister. He didn't say her name or mention what she did for a living. She asked what Jackson liked to do for fun. His explanation of what he enjoyed doing included video games and sports among other things. She wanted to know where Jackson went to college. After he told her that he went to Southern Methodist University, he asked where she had gone to school.

She chuckled and said, "I was far too smart to waste my time in college. I got a job right out of school slinging burgers, from there I graduated to telephone sales. Which, by the way, is not the best career choice for someone who is shy and afraid of rejection. From there I went on to reception work and then moved to customer service, and that's where I've been ever since."

He gave her an abbreviated version of his work history. "After college, I went to work for a family company that specialized in advance programming. My best friend and I had been designing games since we were teens." What he didn't say was that his father once owned the family company. He and Hank eventually took over the business and worked to take it from a moderately profitable company to a multi-billion-dollar leader in the tech industry. They had their hands in every technological product on the market.

"How did you go from that to managing an office?" She asked curiously. "If you and your friend were so into creation, you should have stuck with it."

"I did love creating, but I needed to expand my horizons, and I fell into the support thing, and that's where I've been ever since." He hated lying to her, but it was a necessary evil at this point. He wanted to change the subject before he slipped and said something that might give him away. "When was your last relationship?

83

Victoria swallowed hard. She didn't want to talk about her dating history. To him, it would probably sound pathetic. "It's been a while," she said.

"A month, a year?" He took a bite of the steak on his plate.

"A while," she said sipping the wine he'd chosen for them.

"Longer than a year?" He asked curiously. There was no way this sexy, beautiful woman sitting across from him hadn't been involved with anyone in over a year.

"A lot longer. What about you?" She asked trying to take the focus off herself.

"My last relationship ended a little over a year ago. We didn't want the same things."

"She wanted to get married, and you didn't?"

"Not exactly, she wanted to party and have fun, and I was tired of that. We parted ways, and I'm happy that we did."

"What was she like?" Victoria asked quietly. She wanted to know if his interest in her was a fleeting thing.

"She was younger than me. Pretty by society's standards, but not nearly as beautiful as some." He said winking at her. "She used her looks to manipulate people."

"Tell me what she looked like. You said she was pretty. I'm trying to see what your taste in women is."

Jackson stopped eating and looked directly into her eyes. "My taste at this time in my life is all that matters. I'm attracted to beauty, no different than any other man. I'm tempted by your expressive eyes, cute button nose, soft kissable lips, and every other physical thing about you, that I won't say out loud right now. Most of all I'm attracted to how smart and selfless you are.

The woman, I dated before you, was tall, slim and according to some people, physically flawless. She was selfish and spoiled, but she isn't who I'm sitting here with tonight. You are, and that is my taste exactly." He stood and leaned over the table kissing her briefly. "Since we are going down this road tell me what's your type. I already know you like abs and muscles." He sat back down and resumed eating.

Victoria said she didn't have a type. All she wanted was someone who was a good man. He didn't have to be wealthy or good looking if he loved her and accepted the fact that she and her mother were a package deal, she could be with anyone. Jackson believed her, but he couldn't help but poke fun at her. "So, you're telling me that if I were five feet three and crossed eyes and buck teeth, you'd go out with me?"

After she stopped laughing at the image he'd created she answered, "Yes."

"Bullshit. I had to coerce you to go out with me, and I look a damn sight better than that."

"Okay you've got me there, but with someone like that I wouldn't feel like the beast to his beauty."

"Are you saying that you think I'm beautiful?" He was teasing her.

Victoria blushed and hoped Jackson didn't notice it. She did think he was beautiful, especially looking like he did tonight. He could easily be a model. He was tall, tan and even wearing those nerdy glasses; he was sexy as hell. "I didn't say that."

"I think you did, but it's okay if you need to deny it."

By the time they had finished dinner and cleaning up all the stations, they had discussed family and friendships as well as dating. The one thing they had not talked about was sex, and it was ever present in the back of both their minds.

# Chapter 8 Jackson's Grandfather

Over the next few days Jackson kept his word and did not show any signs of affection in the office, but he took her to dinner on Tuesday and gave her a special kiss when he brought her home. Her mother was sleeping when they arrived, and Jackson spread her open in the chair again and kissed her senseless.

By the time he brought her home on Wednesday Victoria was determined that he wasn't going to get away with just kissing her as he called it. She wanted all he had to offer. Once she checked on her mother and said good night, she took him by the hand and led him through the dining room and kitchen to her bedroom on the opposite side of the house from her mother.

She closed the door and turned on the lamp near the bed. She turned to Jackson and smiled. She slid the straps of the dress she was wearing down her arms. Jackson watched eagerly waiting as she pushed the dress down her body, over her hips and let it fall to the floor at her feet. "I want more than a kiss tonight," she said before touching her lips to his.

She undid the buttons of his shirt running her hands up his tantalizing abs and chest. Jackson's hands quickly found their way to the satiny material covering her plump ass; he grabbed hold picking her up. Victoria wrapped her arms around his shoulder and her legs around his waist. Moving his arm to hold her around her waist, he used his other hand to undo the clasp of her bra.

He was so strong holding her up as she leaned back while he removed her bra and tossed it aside. As soon as the material was gone, he took one breast in his hand flicking his tongue over the hard nipple. He moved to the other one using his fingers to play with the recently abandoned one. Victoria arched her back to give him better access. Her center was on fire with desire. She wanted to feel his hardness pounding her to bliss. She tightened her legs around his waist rubbing herself against the ridge in his pants.

Jackson groaned taking his mouth from her breast. He laid her on the bed and stood between her legs. She watched him as Jackson undid his belt and then his button fly. He watched her as she slid her hand into her panties and played with herself. Jackson didn't think his cock could get any harder than it was. He was wrong. He wanted to go slow and take his time, but she was pushing him with her wanton behavior.

Victoria's finger was slick as she worked her clit. She watched him as he removed his cock and stroked its considerable length. It was thick, and she could see the veins running through it. He ran his hand over the mushroom head spreading the pre-cum. "If you keep that up, I'll have to kiss you later," he said with his eyes focused on the hand in her underwear.

Victoria took her hand out of her panties only to remove them. When she lay naked for his viewing pleasure, she resumed her task. "Fuck me."

Jackson found his pants and got a condom from his wallet. Victoria watched as he opened the packet and slid it on. He pulled her to the edge of the bed by her ankles and rubbed the head of his penis up and down her slick opening. She moaned loving the feel of him against her.

Jackson leaned down sliding his arms under her knees, up her back to grab her by the shoulders. He continued to undulate his hips. As he kissed her, Victoria locked her arms around his neck, and in one smooth move Jackson lifted her off the bed and entered her slowly. Victoria moaned in pleasure. He was big and filled her. It felt good.

Jackson held her without moving for a moment. She was so very tight, and her heat felt as if the condom had become one with his skin. He took his mouth from hers. Her eyes were closed. "Look at me." He demanded. When Victoria met his eyes, he began to move her up and down on him. "You. Are. Mine." He said fiercely punctuating his words with each slow thrust of his hips.

His mouth covered hers again and he moved slowly in and out of her, chanting in his head mine, mine, mine. Victoria held on to Jackson as he started thrusting faster. She could feel the juices running out of her. Victoria had never gotten this wet in her life. She felt the orgasm building quickly in her, and she knew that Jackson was aware of how close she was because he slowed his thrusting and made circular grinding motions deep within her. She pulled her mouth from his squeezing her eyes shut. "Oh God, Yessss! She said as the pleasure took her over the edge.

Jackson could feel her pelvic walls squeezing him as she came. He kept grinding into her he wasn't ready to cum yet. He got onto the bed never severing their connection. She was still twitching on his cock. He kissed her neck and took her hands placing them above her head. He held them there while he slid his other hand between them to rub her clit as he started to push in and out of her again. Her reaction was instantaneous. She had another orgasm.

Victoria wanted to scream out from the pleasure. She bit her lip moaning loudly. She tried to push his hand away because of the intensity, but he held her hands down as he tortured her through her second orgasm. When she thought she was just going to die from cum overload, he removed his hand from between them and let her hands go. He was heavy on top of her, but she liked the weight of him. He reached beneath her with both hands, grabbing her ass and moved faster and faster causing her to explode into another orgasm. He soon joined her moaning, "Tory," over and over again. It was nearly dawn when he left her house, and he did give her a special kiss before he left her home.

Jackson was nearly home when his phone rang. It was Hank. "You're up early." He said when he answered the call.

Hank sounded sleepy when he replied. "Not by choice. I just talked to Beth. She's been trying to reach you for over an hour. Your grandfather is in the hospital."

"What happened? Is he alright? What hospital?" Jackson asked concerned.

"He fell and broke his leg. He's going to be fine. He's at Plano Medical Center."

"Thanks, Hank." Jackson disconnected the call and drove to the hospital.

Thursday morning when Victoria stepped out of her room in the kitchen, her mother was standing by the sink with a cup of coffee. "Morning," Victoria said as she came over to kiss her mother's cheek.

"When are you going to tell me about your new boyfriend?" Her mother asked, adding, "I may not be able to see, but I'm not blind. You've been out three days in a row, and that's different for you."

Victoria hoped her mother wasn't aware that Jackson had been in her room all night. She prayed that she had not heard them getting it on. She was a grown woman, and this was her house, but she didn't want to disrespect her mother. "I didn't tell you anything because I don't think it's that serious."

"What's his name?"

Victoria didn't want to tell her anything about Jackson, but she answered the question. "Jackson."

"Where did you meet him?"

"Momma I have to get ready for work. I'll tell you about him later." She kissed her mother and disappeared out of the kitchen. Victoria didn't want to tell her mother that it was the man who had taken the job she wanted. She also knew that her mom would want to know everything about him and Victoria didn't know that much about him herself.

She was sitting at her desk looking over her workload for the day when Sasha arrived. Sasha walked up to her workspace, "I like this new look you've got going on."

She had been laying wrapped in Jackson's arms as he played with her hair last night when he asked why she always wore her hair pulled back at work. She explained that she felt it looked more professional than her riot of curls and that it was a lot less work to maintain. His response had been to bury his face in her hair and tell her how much he liked the smell and feel of it on his skin. She was wearing it down today to please him.

"Thank you. I thought I'd try something new."

"Well, it looks good. It makes you look younger." Sasha said moving to her desk. "There may be hope for you yet."

"What does that mean?" Victoria snorted as she asked.

"Hope, that we can find you a husband."

"I don't need a husband."

Sasha stood up peeking over the desk to whisper, "Okay maybe just some good old-fashioned sex then." She laughed and sat back down.

Victoria had found that, and she was not about to tell Sasha about it. Throughout the morning she kept eyeing the door waiting for Jackson to enter. After an hour had passed and he hadn't come in yet, she sent him a text.

Victoria: "Where are you?"

She waited trying not to stare at the screen. A few minutes passed and nothing. She went to the front desk. "Millie, have you heard from Jackson this morning?"

Millie was elbow deep in envelopes and sales ads. "Yeah, I'm sorry. I got caught up in this mess and forgot to tell you. He said he wouldn't be in today. His grandfather is in the hospital."

Victoria hoped his grandfather was okay. She went back to her desk and sent another text.

Victoria: Millie told me you wouldn't be in today.
If there's anything I can do, let me know.

For the rest of the morning, she continued to check her phone for a return message.


Jackson Edward Coates sat on the hospital bed watching Magnum P.I. on the wall-mounted television while his grandson slept in the chair beside him. He had shown up early this morning and sent Beth home. The older Jackson had been resting when something buzzed on the bed beside him. It was his grandson's phone. Since his grandson was asleep, he picked it up and read the message from Victoria Timmons. He didn't know who Victoria was but, there was something she could do. He sent a reply to her.

Jackson hadn't meant to fall asleep, but he was tired after

having been up all night. He smiled as he thought of how delicious Victoria had looked when he left her this morning. She had thrown on a large t-shirt and sweatpants. Her hair was wild and bushy. It had been hard not to stay with her.

"What's got you smiling like the cat that swallowed the canary?" His grandfather asked from the bed beside him. Jackson didn't answer he just smiled even brighter. "Oh, it's a woman. Who is she?"

"I didn't say it was a woman," Jackson said sitting up to stretch his back out.

"You didn't have to. Your grandmother used to make me smile like that. By the way, someone named Victoria has been texting you. I told her you were sleeping."

Jackson grabbed his phone reading the text from his grandfather. Grandpa Jack had introduced himself and asked Victoria to bring them some lunch preferably good Mexican food. He had texted her that eating hospital food was worse pain than his broken leg. She had agreed and said she wouldn't have him suffering two types of pain and would be happy to bring lunch.

Jackson looked at the time of the last text and the current time. It was almost noon. She was probably on her way there now. He hoped he had enough time to explain the situation to his grandfather. "I need to tell you something, and I don't have much time."

"I'm listening," his grandfather said.

Before Jackson could tell him anything, Victoria knocked on the door and poked her head inside. "Hi." She came in with a large blue bag with Favor written on it. She unzipped it and pulled out a paper bag from Mi Cocina.

Jackson smiled as Victoria came in, sitting the bag on the

rolling table next to the bed. She was wearing her hair down. She looked beautiful in the close-fitting black dress that stopped just below her knee, and she was wearing high heels. "Grandfather this is Victoria Timmons, Victoria, my grandfather." He watched as his grandfather sat up a little straighter smoothing the sheets and blankets before running his hand through his longish gray hair to make himself presentable.

"The name is Jackson Coates. It's a pleasure to meet you." His grandfather said extending his hand to her.

Victoria took his hand. "Likewise. So, he's named after you." Jackson watched as his grandfather kissed the back of her hand. The old fart was hitting on his girl. Once he let go of her hand, Victoria pulled several containers from the bag along with napkins and plastic ware. "I hope you like enchiladas, Mr. Coates. I bought chicken and beef and some Spanish rice and refried beans."

"I like her a lot. You, my darling can call me Jackson." his grandfather said rubbing his hands together.

Jackson smiled at his grandfather's antics. "Call him Grandpa Jack."

Victoria produce two cups, placing them in front of his grandfather. "I wasn't sure what you might like to drink, so I got raspberry tea and an Arnold Palmer. You can have what you like, and Jackson can have the other." She said pointing to him.

"Jackson? Why..." Grandpa Jack said looking at his grandson.

"I'll take the raspberry tea," Jackson said interrupting him and shaking his head no, slightly at his grandfather before he finished his question. He knew that his grandfather would ask, why is she calling you Jackson. Everyone called him

Max.

Victoria opened the containers, and once Jackson's grandfather had chosen the chicken enchiladas, she handed the other to Jackson. Before Jackson's grandfather started to eat, he asked, "Aren't you going to join us for lunch?"

"I'll grab a salad or something on the way back to the office." She said zipping up her Favor bag.

"Nonsense, I won't eat all of this. You can share with me." Grandpa Jack used the lid as a dish, sliding one of his enchiladas, then some rice and beans onto it.

"No, really I can't," Victoria said putting the bag on her shoulder. "I should get back to work."

"I'm sure your boss wouldn't mind. Would you?" He said looking at his grandson.

Jackson smiled at them both. "Of course not. Please join us." He knew from the look on his grandfather's face that he was curious about why Victoria had called him Jackson, and he intended to have some fun at his expense.

"See, he's fine with it. Jackson pull that chair over here for her to sit next to me. It's been a long time since I've enjoyed the company of such a beautiful young lady." He said as Jackson moved the other chair in the room to the other side of the bed. Victoria still looked unsure. He slid the bag from her shoulder, placing it on the floor beside the chair.

Victoria sat and took the food Jackson's grandfather handed her. "Thank you."

Jackson returned to his chair. His grandfather talked to and flirted with Victoria as they ate. "Tell me, darling, what is it that you do?"

Victoria was chewing so Jackson filled in the answer hoping that his grandfather would not ask anything that might give him away. "Victoria handles a lot of things at the company. I don't think a specific title would do for her."

"Jackson gives me too much credit." She said in between bites.

"I doubt it. Have you worked for Jackson for a long time?" Grandpa Jack asked emphasizing his name while looking at his grandson and raising an eyebrow.

"No, it's only been a short time," Victoria said in between bites.

"I hope Jackson's not working you too hard. Jackson can be single minded in his focus on business."

"No sir, he doesn't. I'm just hardworking by nature." Victoria smiled at Jackson's grandfather, then winked at Jackson. She noticed that Jackson's grandfather said his name a lot and with some inflection each time he said it.

"Surely, you're not making her work late every night, Jackson?" He asked smiling wickedly at his grandson. "I'm sure her husband and family would like to have her home in the evenings."

Jackson knew that his grandfather was fishing for information, for what, he wasn't sure. He was also making sure that Jackson knew, that he was aware that there was something secretive going on in this room. His constant act of calling him Jackson said it all.

"I'm not married, so there is no husband to object," Victoria said smiling at both men.

"Beautiful and single, this must be my lucky day." Grandpa Jack teased her. "If you don't have a boyfriend, I may have to take you dancing when my leg is all better."

Jackson watched Victoria as he ate. She was enjoying his grandfather's flirting. She blushed and said. "That sounds like fun."

Victoria liked Jackson's grandfather. He was openly flirting with her, but it was sweet. She was confident that he didn't mean anything by it.

"Do you have a boyfriend or significant other? I know I'm nosy, but I need to know if I will have to fight for your affection."

Victoria finished her food while thinking of what to say. She and Jackson were just starting to date, and she didn't want to complicate things by putting labels on their relationship, and he apparently hadn't told his grandfather that they were dating.

"She has a boyfriend grandpa, and I don't think he would like that you are trying to steal his girl from him," Jackson said before she could answer. Victoria stopped what she was doing, looking at Jackson who met her gaze. He, however, had no problem putting a label on their relationship and he was making sure that she knew it.

"Well, I guess I'll just have to keep looking for the next Mrs. Jackson Coates." Grandpa Jack hadn't missed the exchange between the two of them after his grandson said she had a boyfriend.

Jackson's phone rang. He checked the caller ID. It was Hank. "I'm going to take this in the hall. No business talk while I'm gone." He said as he left the room. Hopefully, nothing would be said that he'd regret while he was out of the room.

Jackson stepped out into the hallway. "What's up?" he

asked. Hank told him that they still hadn't found out who his father was with, but that Hank's investigators had discovered that his mother was correct. His father was paying for an apartment, car and had been withdrawing money from his account in large sums. "Cut off his access to everything. If he wants a dime, he'll have to get it from me, and whoever he is screwing will soon let us know who she is when she realizes the well is running dry."

Victoria took the containers from their finished meal putting them back into the Mi Cocina bag to dispose of on her way out. "So, you and my grandson are seeing each other?" Jackson's grandfather asked almost as soon as the door closed.

Victoria didn't want to lie to him but since Jackson had said she was his girlfriend she didn't see the harm in telling the truth. "Yes sir." Victoria didn't want to talk about her and Jackson. "How long are they going to have you here?"

"I should be going home today. I bumped my head too, so they wanted to make sure I didn't have a concussion. I'll be fine. The problem I'll have is that I won't get to have you bring me food once I go home."

Victoria smiled at him. She reached into her favor bag and pulled out a business card and a pen. She wrote her cell phone number on the back of the card handing it to him. "This is my number, you can call me anytime. I'd be happy to bring you whatever you need."

Grandpa Jack looked at the card. "What is Favor?"

Victoria explained that Favor was an on-demand delivery

service and that she was an independent contractor in business for herself. He was tickled to find out that he could have just about anything delivered to his home for a fee. He asked her to install the application on his phone and tuck her card into his pants pocket hanging in the closet. She found his phone in the drawer of the table next to his bed. She also programmed her phone number into the phone telling him that he didn't have to submit a request through Favor, she would be happy to bring him whatever he needed while he was recuperating.

Just as Jackson came back into the room, Victoria said, "I really should get back to the office. It was a pleasure meeting you, and I hope you are all better soon."

"The pleasure was all mine, I assure you." He replied smiling brightly at her.

"I'll walk you to the elevator," Jackson said from the foot of his grandfather's bed. "I'll be right back grandpa." He put the Favor bag on his shoulder so that she could carry her purse and he grabbed the bag with the food containers.

Jackson followed Victoria into the hall. Once they were far enough from the door, he slipped his hand into hers. "Thank you for bringing lunch."

"You're welcome. I like your grandfather." She said as they reached the elevator. She pushed the button.

"He likes you too. A little too much I think." He slipped the bag onto her shoulder as he kissed her. "You are my girlfriend, so he will just have to find his own." He said as the elevator doors opened. Victoria stepped in without saying a word. When she pushed the button, Jackson was still standing there smiling at her as the doors closed.

# Chapter 9 Tete-A-Tete

"Alright Maximillion Jackson Quinn," his grandfather said as he entered the room emphasizing his middle name. "What the hell is going on? Why are you lying to the lovely young lady?" His grandfather added.

"Grandpa it's complicated." He said sitting in the chair that Victoria had used. He sighed heavily then smiled.

"So, she's the one you were smiling about when you woke up."

It wasn't a question, but Jackson answered anyway. "Yes."

"Let me guess; you are the boyfriend that won't like me trying to steal his girl?" His grandfather asked rubbing his chin the same way Jackson did when he was thinking.

"Yes, and she doesn't know who I am," Jackson said getting up and walking around the bed to the window. Jackson looked out the window while he explained to his grandfather about the deal that he had made with Peter Albrecht, and the last week and a half that he had been undercover at the company.

"How do you expect this to end?" Grandpa Jack asked after hearing his grandson out.

"I don't know." He said honestly turning to face his grandfather. "I didn't expect this to happen. I think she is amazing. I tried to stay away from her, but..." He paused trying to find the right way to explain himself.

"But what? Do you love her?"

Jackson took a deep breath. "We've only known each other for a few weeks, and it's only been a few days since our first date. It's too soon to say that, I think."

"This is not going to end well you know. When Victoria finds out who you are and that you've been lying to her about it, she's going to tear you a new one."

"I know," Jackson said sliding into the chair again. "I can't tell her who I am until after the purchase goes through."

"Well sounds to me like you've got one hell of a problem. I remember the time I lied to your grandmother when we were dating. Let's just say that I learned my lesson really quick." Grandpa Jack said laying his head back on the pillow.

"What did you lie to her about?"

"Something like your current situation. When we met I let Margaret believe that I was from a well to do family. I just happen to have the same surname, but I wasn't related to them at all."

"How did she find out?" Jackson asked curiously. He had never heard this story before.

"Well, this family was having a big party, one that was in the society pages. Not that I knew anything about it. I didn't keep up with that kind of thing. Margaret waited and waited for me to invite her, and when I didn't, she stopped taking my calls and wouldn't see me." He sat up looking Jackson in the eye. "It took a month of me trying to see her before I finally caught her away from her friends and family.

I found her coming out of the library and begged her to hear me out. She yelled at me, saying that I could just go straight to hell. She believed that I didn't invite her because she was poor and that I was ashamed of her." Grandpa Jack snorted. "She was so mad that she threw a book at me, a big book and she was using the foulest language. Sailors would have cringed at the names she called me."

"What did you say to get her to come around?" Jackson asked. It was hard for him to picture his grandma Margie cussing and throwing things. She had always been sweet and loving.

He laughed. "I kissed her, just to get her to stop talking. She was so stunned it took a second to sink in. She kissed me back and then when I let her go, she slapped me, but I had her attention. I told her the truth, that I was dirt poor and that I wanted to impress her and that I was not related to the wealthy Coates family. I told her that I loved her and that I wouldn't marry her until I could give her all the things she deserved."

"Well, you held up your end of that promise." Jackson said and added, "She married you, and you made a success of yourself."

"Yes, I did, but I could have lost her. You, my boy, must decide how important she is to you and if what your doing is worth the pain that you're going to cause her. No matter what you do son, she is going to find out who you are, and she is going to be hurt by it. It would be better to tell her sooner rather than later, no matter how serious you are about her." Jackson nodded his head acknowledging his grandfather's words. "If she breaks up with you, how long is appropriate before I ask her out?" Grandpa Jack grinned wickedly at his grandson.

Jackson gave his grandpa the evil eye. "Do you want me to break the other leg?" Jackson said playfully. His grandfather laughed at him. Grandpa Jack knew from that statement that his grandson was more serious about Victoria than he thought.

Jackson sat chatting with him about random things before

his grandfather's doctor released him. Jackson insisted that he stay with him instead of going home alone.

He sent a text Victoria before they left the hospital.

Jackson: "My grandpa is getting released today, and he's going to stay with me for a while. I want to see you tonight."

Victoria: "That would be nice, but you should stay home and take care of your grandpa. Besides I need to go workout."

Jackson: "I can give you a much better workout than you can get in the gym."

Victoria: "I know you can, but I still need to go and I need to get back to work."

Jackson sent her a kissing emoji.

Grandpa Jack could have gone home. He lived on the family estate in a smallish house far enough away from the main house that he didn't have to deal with the pretentious behavior of his son-in-law. Doug or Douglas as he liked to be called now, hadn't been that way when Douglas met his sweet daughter Kelly. He had seemed to be down to earth and practical until his business began to make a lot of money and it was even worse now that they were filthy rich.

He decided to stay with his grandson because he was formulating a plan, a plan that might lead to great-grandchildren. If he kept waiting for either of his grandchildren to settle down, he'd never get to have any. Beth was as involved with the business as Hank and Max, and she was a modern woman who felt that she could put off having kids or maybe she didn't want to have any at all. If he hoped to bounce great-grandchildren on his lap before he died, he was going to have to take matters into his own hands.

Once Jackson got his grandfather up to his penthouse, he got him settled into the bedroom on the main floor and went to his room to shower and change. His housekeeper had gotten Grandpa Jack's room ready and had prepared dinner for them. He was expecting Hank in an hour or so. They had some things to discuss, and he was bringing paperwork that required his signature.

Jackson got dressed and made his way downstairs. Hank was sitting at the table with his grandfather. Maria, his live-in housekeeper, was bringing a plate from the kitchen for him. "Thank you, Maria." He said taking the plate from her hand.

"Do you need anything else?"

"No. I think we will be fine." He joined the men at the table. He sat down at the head of the table between Hank who sat on his left and his grandfather on his right.

"Grandpa Jack was just telling me about your girlfriend. He said she's beautiful and that you threatened him for flirting with her." Hank said cutting into the steak in front of him, watching Jackson's face. He was, of course, having a little fun at his friend's expense. Grandpa Jack was probably wrong about this woman being Jackson's girlfriend, someone he was sleeping with maybe, but not his girlfriend.

Jackson put his napkin in his lap picking up his steak knife and fork. "Hello Hank, how are you?"

Hank smiled. "I'm great."

"Tell him about her, Jackson," Grandpa Jack said eating a spoonful of mashed potatoes.

"Jackson?" Hank said looking from one to the other.

"She calls him Jackson." Grandpa Jack added with a smirk.

"What the..." Hank said dropping his utensils with a clang. "Don't tell me it's someone from Albrecht." He couldn't believe his ears. "You are supposed to be doing evaluations, not the employees."

Jackson wanted to choke his grandfather. "It's not what you think." He said to Hank.

"Then what is it?" His best friend asked leaning back in his chair. Grandpa Jack sat watching them as he ate his dinner. He waited along with Hank to hear his grandson explain the situation. Grandpa Jack was hoping that he would admit that this young lady meant more to him than just a sexual conquest. He needed to know how serious his feelings were before he proceeded with his plan.

"I don't have to justify my actions to either of you, but I like her," Jackson said taking a drink from the water glass next to his plate.

"You like her," Hank repeated his words sarcastically. "He likes her Grandpa Jack."

"I heard him." Jackson's grandfather said with a chuckle.

"How do you think she's going to react when she finds out who you are? More importantly, how do you think she is going to react when you shut down the company that she works for?"

"Alright already," Jackson said. He knew that he would have to deal with the situation he had put himself in, but he didn't need to have Hank smack him in the face with it. "I don't know what I was thinking."

"I know what you were thinking with," Hank said running his hand down his face in frustration. "You can't ruin this deal man."

I know. I remember what's at stake here, but..." Jackson said to Hank.

"But nothing. We need that software and the only way to get it was to concede to Albrecht's demands to try to save his employees. You signed the confidentiality agreement too. Neither you nor Albrecht can say a word about this until it's all said and done legally. So, you either have to break it off with her, or you have to ride it out, but you can't tell her the truth until I give you the all clear. You got that?" Hank wanted Jackson to say it.

Jackson looked him in the eye. "I got it." Jackson couldn't tell Victoria about his deal with Peter. That hadn't changed, but he wasn't going to stop seeing her either. Hank was right she would probably never speak to him again after the deal went through. Of all the employees in the office he was sure that he would find a place for her at Q.E., but would she take it once she knew everything and would she break it off with him.

He should never have kissed her that night at the bar, hell he shouldn't have asked her to have a drink with him at all. He tried to tell himself that it was just a physical attraction, but he knew it was more than that. She wasn't like his previous girlfriends; she was working hard to achieve something worthwhile. She wanted to succeed in business on her own. She wasn't counting on her beauty to carry her through life. She wasn't shallow and superficial. She was one of a kind.

Grandpa Jack finished his meal watching his grandson. He could see the internal conflict waging war within him. Jackson apparently had feelings for Victoria. Maybe he hadn't realized what they were, but he was working it out.

After they finished their meal, Grandpa Jack said goodnight to Hank and his grandson and retired to the guest room off the kitchen leaving them to discuss their other business dealings.

# Chapter 10 The Flowers

Victoria lay on her bed after her shower. She was tired and sore, tired from not getting enough sleep the night before and sore from the workout she put herself through tonight, mostly. She could attribute some of her soreness to the exercise Jackson had given her the night before. She smiled to herself as she thought about it. She had bubbles in her belly again thinking about him.

She had a hard time all day containing the bubbly feeling in her gut. Every time she thought about him her heart beat faster. Meeting his grandfather was an unexpected treat. She yawned and reached for the latest romance she was reading. Her phone buzzed indicating a new text message. She checked her phone.

Jackson: "Thinking of you. What are you doing?"

Victoria: "In bed reading, what are you doing?"

Jackson: "What are you wearing?"

Victoria: "T-shirt."

Jackson: "Show me."

Victoria giggled before replying.

Victoria: "You want a picture?"

Jackson: "Yes."

Victoria took a selfie and sent it to him. She was propped up against the headboard. Her hair was loose and spread out on the pillow. She smiled and made sure he could see the words on her shirt.

Jackson received the picture and burst out laughing. Her shirt said, "If you're ugly, please leave before I wake up." He loved it.

Jackson: "I love it. Is that what you sleep in most of the time?"

Victoria: "I have lots of t-shirts with crazy sayings on them."

Jackson: "Are you wearing anything under it?"

Victoria blushed before sending a message back.

Victoria: "Wouldn't you like to know?"

Jackson read Victoria's message and smiled. She was teasing him, well two could play that game.

Jackson: "Yes. Show me."

A few seconds later he got a picture that showed she was naked underneath her t-shirt.

Before he could send anything else, she sent another message.

Victoria: "Now show me what you're wearing."

Jackson smiled and sent her a picture.

Victoria liked this game they were playing. He sent her a picture that made her mouth water. She downloaded it to her phone and put in a private folder that required a password to see it. A few minutes later her phone rang. "Hello." She answered.

"I wish I were there with you," Jackson said low and

seductively. He went on to tell her what he would do to her if he was there and was pleased when he asked if she was touching herself. When she said she was, he stroked his cock and told her, "Do what I tell you to. I want to hear you cum."

Victoria listened and did as Jackson instructed. Phone sex was something she had done once before. Phone sex had seemed silly to her when Victoria tried it the first time, but with Jackson it was erotic. She moved her fingers the way he told her to. When she slid her hand between her thighs, Victoria found that she was extremely wet and when she rubbed her clit, it was swollen and sensitive.

She could tell that he was stroking himself at the same time. His breathing had changed. He told her how he wanted her to touch herself. His breath was slow at times, and at others, it was faster. She was breathing similarly to him. They came almost at the same time, and it was almost as intense as when he was physically with her.

Jackson spoke first, "I love the sounds you make." Victoria giggled slightly embarrassed by what she had just done. She couldn't say anything as she lay there smiling. He also loved that she seemed shy after their intimate moments. "Get some sleep."

"Night." Victoria didn't have the strength to say much else. Once Jackson disconnected the call, she slid out of bed and went to clean up.

The next morning as she pulled into the parking lot at work her phone rang. It was Jackson's grandfather. "Hello."

"Good morning. I hope I'm not bothering you too early." He said cheerfully.

"Of course not."

110

"I was wondering if you might be free for lunch one day next week. I'd like to repay you for your kindness. I do have one condition though."

"What condition?" Victoria was curious enough to ask.

"My grandson can't know about it." She wanted to ask why that was important, but he filled in the answer saying, "I need help with a present for him, and I thought you might be able to help me."

"I don't think that will be a problem. Let me figure out what day would be best next week, and I'll call you back later today."

"Fine darling, that will be perfect." Victoria ended the call and got out of the car.

"That's two days in a row," Millie said as she entered the office.

"Two days in a row?" Victoria asked, not understanding what she meant.

Millie pointed to her hair. "Two days in a row that you've worn it down. What's up with that?"

Victoria touched her curly locks, "I've been getting headaches. I think my head needs a break." Victoria walked through the office to her desk. Sam spoke to her and went back to whatever he was doing. Victoria put her purse away and turned her computer on.

It seemed that Victoria wearing her hair down two days in a row was the talk of the office. She received a lot of compliments. The only one that mattered came as a text message.

Jackson: "Wear your hair down tonight."

Victoria: "Don't forget, I have to cover the phones tonight."

Jackson: "We can have a late dinner."

Victoria: "Cool."

Jackson spent the day talking with the people on the finance team and trying not to think about Victoria and what he wanted to do to her later. He went to lunch with Eugene, Tanner, Jim, and George, who worked with Eugene and Tanner in programming. He learned that Jim was the only one who didn't have a crush on his woman.

When the talk at the table segued to women, Tanner told them that when he first came to work there, he had wanted to ask Victoria out, but he was too shy and intimidated by her. Eugene admitted that he had a thing for her also. They were both married now, thanks to Sasha fixing them up. George had asked her out. She had turned him down sweetly.

He couldn't blame them for their infatuation with her. He had fallen under her spell the same as they had. The only difference was she had given him a chance to get to know her outside the office. He thought about his promise to Hank last night. She had taken a chance on him, and he had no idea if things were going to work out once he told her who he was, and why he did it. She would probably tell him to go straight to hell.

As Victoria and Sasha came back from lunch, Millie stopped them at the front desk. "Hey, you got flowers today." Sasha reached for the flowers. Millie swatted her hands away. "Not you."

"Me?" Victoria asked looking for a card in the bouquet. They were beautiful. She wasn't sure what kind of flowers they were, but they were beautiful. Some were red, and some were lavender colored. She found the card, praying that Jackson had not signed his name to the card. They could only be from him.

"Your elegance and dignity are examples of your rare and delicate beauty." was all the card said.

"Well, who are they from?" Sasha asked nosily.

"Yeah," Millie added.

Victoria handed her the card and sniffed the flowers. They smelled wonderful. Sasha read the card and gave it to Millie. "Who is it?"

Victoria took her card from Millie, picked up her flowers and said, "I don't know, but they are beautiful." She went to her desk with Sasha hot on her heels.

"What do you mean you don't know?"

"I don't know," Victoria said moving some things around on her desk to make room for her gift.

Sasha didn't believe that Victoria didn't know who the flowers were from, but she could see that she wasn't going to get any answers from Victoria. She left her alone and went back to work.

Jackson noticed the flowers immediately. He stopped at her desk. "Nice flowers."

Victoria smiled. "Yes, they are."

From over the wall, Sasha spoke. "She won't tell me who they're from."

"Is that right?" He said looking at Sasha, Victoria and then the flowers.

Victoria smiled, "I can't tell what I don't know."

"You have a secret admirer," Jackson said slowly.

"I guess so." She said shrugging her shoulders. Victoria watched as Jackson went into his office. A minute later she got a text alert.

Jackson: "Who are they from?"

Victoria: "Aren't they from you?"

Jackson: "No."

Victoria: "Wow, then I have no idea who sent them."

Jackson: "Wasn't there a card?"

Victoria: "Yes but it had no name on it."

Jackson didn't send any more messages. Victoria was curious about this turn of events. If Jackson didn't send them, then who? She'd probably never know, but she was going to enjoy them.

After a quiet dinner in a romantic little bistro, Jackson suggested they go to the lake. He drove around for a while until he found a spot unoccupied by others. He got out and opened her door for her. She slipped her hand into his. They walked away from the car to a picnic table. Victoria hopped up on the end of the table. Jackson stood a foot from her. He reached out caressing her face.

"What's on your mind?" Victoria asked him, taking his hand and pulling him closer.

He stood between her thighs, looking down at her. He didn't want to tell her that he was still upset about the flowers. He didn't want to sound jealous, but he was. "I don't like the idea that someone wants what's mine."

"You mean the flowers?" She was tickled and slightly annoyed that he kept referring to her as his. The most feminine part of her liked being claimed by him, but the modern woman wanted to set him straight. They hadn't been dating for long, and to her, this was not going to last very long anyway. She liked him. She especially loved the sex, but she realized that the difference in their ages would become an issue if they continued to see each other.

He was a young man, and he would at some point realize that he wanted to get married and have children. She was nearing the age when that might not be a possibility. She was ten years older than him. Right now, everything was great, but what would happen when he thought about their age difference. He called her his, but only for now. If now was all she could have with him, she was going to live and love every moment of it.

"Yes." He said wanting to add that he didn't like that the men in their office all admitted to wanting her too. He was thinking irrationally, and he knew it. She was here with him, and she hadn't expressed any interest in any other man.

"Look, I honestly don't know who sent them. I thought it was you. It could have been from a customer or something. That has happened before. It could be their way of showing their appreciation for me fixing their issue." She looked around the area. "Now tell me why you brought me out here? You're not planning to murder me and throw my body in the lake, are you?" She laughed teasing him.

"No, I'm not planning to kill you and throw your body in the lake, but I do plan to have my way with you." He said before grabbing her at the back of her head by her hair, tilting her head back and taking her mouth forcefully. Victoria reached for him pulling him into the cradle of her thighs, wrapping her arms around him. Jackson let her hair go pushing her to lay on the table top. He released her mouth and kissed her chin and neck. Jackson pulled her shirt up above her breasts. He kissed her soft brown skin as he pushed the satin material of her bra up exposing her nipples.

Victoria squirmed beneath him, not caring that anyone could come along and see them while he sucked and licked her nipples, she opened her eyes arching her neck to watch him. He moaned as he went back and forth tasting them. Victoria reached between them undoing his belt buckle. When she had his pants open, she reached inside rubbing his hardness. "Is that what you want?" He asked her before kissing her mouth again.

"Yes." She said when he let her mouth go. He set her on the ground undoing her jeans and spinning her around. He pulled her pants down to her knees and pushed her shoulders so that she lay bent over the table. His mouth watered when he looked at her enticing round backside. She was wearing a thong.

Victoria lay there as he ran his tongue across each cheek, then he hooked his thumbs under the thong and slowly pulled it down to meet her jeans. He placed kisses down the center. He spread her open slightly rubbing his finger against her wet lips. She quaked as she felt his breath cooling the heat of her core. He kissed her before sliding his tongue over her swelling clit. She groaned while he teased her, waiting for him to give her what she wanted.

Jackson sucked her into his mouth. She tasted sweet, and

he devoured her, licking and sucking her until she exploded, her wetness oozing onto his tongue. He stood, took the condom from his pocket covering himself. He rubbed his cock against her, grabbing her hips before slamming into her. He intended to make sure that she knew that she belonged to him. He didn't move for a moment. She felt incredible.

She squirmed wanting him to move. When he started the thrust deep into her, she gave him a command. "Spank me."

He smacked one cheek and felt her clench around him, and she moaned with pleasure. He slapped the other cheek. "You like that?" He didn't wait for an answer. He could tell by the involuntary spasm she was having around him. He rubbed her ass to soothe the sting before he smacked each cheek again as he slammed into her again.

"Yes, yes, yes." She loved the sting as he smacked her over and over as another orgasm rushed to release itself. He could tell she was close, and so was he. "Tell me you love my cock, Tori." He demanded.

She didn't hesitate. "I love your cock, baby. Make me cum." He thrust into her and slid his hand around to rub her clit. As soon as he touched her engorged nub, she clenched and exploded as he went over the edge too. He bent kissing her back as he withdrew himself from her. She lay there for a moment. She couldn't stand just yet. He removed the condom and fixed his clothes before sliding her thong and jeans into place.

Jackson was breathing hard. He smacked her ass again as he plopped down on the bench. His legs were unsteady. He watched her as she slowly stood and fixed her shirt, buttoned and zipped her pants. He wanted her again, but it was amazing that they had not been interrupted. He was sure that wouldn't work out for them a second time, but he was almost willing to risk it.

Jackson took Victoria back to her car, which they had left at the restaurant. He told her he wanted to go back to her house, but she told him to go home and check on Grandpa Jack. After watching her drive away, Jackson went home. His grandfather was sleeping when he returned.

He was sitting in his office staring at his computer screen but hadn't gotten anything done. He was thinking about Victoria. He wished he could bring her here, make love to her all night long and wake up with her in his arms.

That couldn't happen until he told her the truth and it may not happen after that. He rubbed his chin. The month-long evaluations would be completed in two weeks, and then it was just a matter of getting the paperwork for the sale signed, and then Hank would give him the okay. He had to come up with a way to explain his actions.

Jackson spent the weekend working on other Q.E. business. When he wasn't focused on that, he was thinking of Victoria. Jackson tried not to bother her too much. He knew that she was working her other job. He hated that she had to work two jobs. If she knew who he was, and they were dating openly, he could tell her to quit her second job, and he would make sure that she had anything she needed.

Maria knocked on his door around noon on Saturday. "Mr. Quinn, the concierge, just rang, Mr. and Mrs. Quinn are on their way up."

"Thanks, Maria." Jackson had spoken with his mother earlier and knew that she and his father were coming to visit her father sometime today. He would give his mother a moment or two to fuss over his grandfather before joining them in the living room.

Jackson's grandfather was sitting in the living area with his foot propped up on a pillow watching something on one of the sports channels, probably college football when Maria opened the door for Douglas and Kelly. Kelly entered and whipped her gold-colored silk Pashmina off, handing it to Maria before going to her father. "Dad, how are you?"

Grandpa Jack used the remote to mute the volume on the television. He knew that he would not be able to continue enjoying the game until Doug and Kelly left. "Hi, sweetheart." He said as she kissed his forehead.

She sat in the chair near the sofa. "Why didn't you call us when this happened?"

Grandpa Jack sighed, "You were in New York. What could you have done? There was no need to ruin your trip."

Doug walked to the bar and poured a snifter of brandy. "While we appreciate your thoughtful gesture, we should have heard this from you or the staff at the house. Instead, we didn't find out about this until Beth called to tell us you were staying here when they released you from the hospital."

Grandpa Jack was explaining why he had instructed the staff not to contact his parents when Jackson entered the room. His mother rose, and air kissed his cheeks. "Wow, what is this new look you've got going. I like it. I was never one for that beard of yours. You are far too handsome to cover this face with hair." She said shaking his face by the chin.

His father was sitting in the opposite armchair from his mother. "Hello, Dad." Jackson acknowledge his father with a nod of his head. "How was the trip?"

Jackson sat listening to his father talk about his parents' recent trip to New York. His father said it was a mini vacation his mother had insisted they take. Jackson knew it was. His father's way of getting his mother to forget that he had screwed up again.

According to his father, she had wanted to take in a Broadway show and find some new art for one of the rooms she was redecorating on their estate. This trip also allowed his father the chance to shop for antiques, something that had become a new passion since his retirement.

His father finally finished talking about his latest acquisition, a painting that his father was almost sure that Johannes Vermeer painted. If he were correct, the art could be worth millions. Jackson's mother had been fussing over his grandfather, fluffing his pillows and when he tried to escape to his bedroom, she had followed him.

She returned just as his father was finishing his account of how he stumbled onto the location of this possible Vermeer painting. "Dad says you have a new girlfriend. Is she the reason for the new look you've got?" She said as she came to join them in the living room.

He quickly explained that his darker hair and clean-shaven face was because of business. That it had nothing to do with the woman he was seeing. "This is because I'm spying on the employees of a company I'm about to buy."

His mother wasn't about to let go of the fact that there was a new woman in his life. "Well who is she dear and when will we get to meet her?"

"Kelly, leave him alone. More than likely this is some passing fancy of his that will be gone as quickly as she came. Is the company the one that has the security software? Hank mentioned it to me when I spoke with him last week." His father asked with enthusiasm.

"Dad, it's going to change everything for us. The software can be adapted across all of our product lines." Jackson and his father talked business for a while. His mother sat listening but didn't make any comments on the subject.

Kelly wasn't interested in the business talk going on. She was looking at her son. He seemed different, not just in appearance. He looked relaxed. He was smiling more. He always seems so serious to her. His mind was always on the next big deal, and it seemed that much had not changed. Then it hit her, he was happy. When he smiled, it reached his eyes. Maybe it was because of this woman her father mentioned. Was her son in love?

She smiled at the thought. That was all she wanted for her children. She wanted them both to be happy and find someone they could share their lives with. They were doing well in business, it was time to think of other things, and she wanted grandchildren almost as much as her father wanted great-grandchildren.

Beth was the epitome of a modern woman, she had a successful career and was beautiful with a lovely body, but she was headstrong, and it would take a strong man to win her heart. Her son needed someone strong as well, someone who would stand up to him. He tended to be pushy when he wanted something. Hopefully, this woman he was seeing was a good match for him. She broke up the business talk and told her husband she was ready to go home.

# Chapter 11 Lunch with Grandpa Jack

Victoria waited until Jackson was in the conference room with the sales team and a potential client before leaving to have lunch with grandpa Jack. She had offered to pick him up, but he insisted on meeting her at Lucky's on Oaklawn Avenue. She was walking away from her desk when Sasha stopped her. "Where are you off to?"

"I'm having lunch with a friend. I'll be back in an hour or so." She said over her shoulder. She hoped that Grandpa Jack didn't have too hard of a time getting around on the crutches. She felt terrible that she hadn't been able to convince him to allow her to bring lunch to him, but he insisted that he was tired of being inside and wanted to get out.

He was already there when she arrived. "Hi, I hope you haven't been waiting too long."

"Not at all. You look fabulous." He said as she kissed his cheek before sitting opposite him at the table.

"Thank you." She said just before the waitress appeared to take their order.

Grandpa Jack had an agenda today. He had to sneak out of the house. He had told Maria to bring lunch to his room. He said he would take a nap after he ate and for her not to bother him. When she had returned to her quarters, he ordered a car service, and as quickly as he could, he left the apartment.

After the waitress had gotten their order down on her pad and was walking away, he said, "I'm an old man, and I don't know how much time I have left on this earth. I want to ask you some questions, and they may be none of my business, but I'm hoping you will indulge me."

"Grandpa Jack, what's going on?" Victoria asked in surprise.

"I know that you and my grandson are dating. You've told me that. What I want to know from you is, what are your feelings for my grandson?"

Victoria looked him in the eye. She was still discovering what she felt. She wasn't ready to answer this question yet, not even to herself. "I'm not sure how I feel. We haven't known each other long."

"He said pretty much the same thing." He said shaking his head. "Let's start with the basics. You are attracted to him. You like him enough to spend time with him." They weren't questions; they were statements of fact. He smiled as Victoria nodded her head. "In this day and age, I'm sure that you two are being intimate." The flush of color to her cheeks was answer enough. "I'm not judging. His grandmother and I knew each other in the biblical sense before our wedding day."

Victoria sat and listened to Grandpa Jack as he told her about his beloved Maggie and their courtship. It was a beautiful story that Grandpa Jack told lovingly. He had finished his tale by the time their food arrived. Then grandpa Jack talked to her about how lovely it was to see the weather starting to change. He liked fall and in Dallas fall sometimes didn't begin until around Thanksgiving which was a few weeks away. "Kelly, my daughter will be serving a delicious dinner. I'm sure my grandson will invite you, that is if you don't already have plans."

Victoria smiled at the thought of spending Thanksgiving with Grandpa Jack and Jackson's family. "That sounds like a nice idea, but I had planned to cook dinner for my mother and me."

Grandpa Jack was not deterred. "We, of course, you would bring your mother too. I'd like to meet her, and if she is a charming as you are, I'm sure she and I will hit it off famously."

Victoria thought it was sweet of Grandpa Jack to invite her to their family gathering but would that be okay with Jackson. It was kind of early for them to be spending the holidays together. She told herself not to think about it too much.

By the time they finished their food, Victoria had realized that Grandpa Jack hadn't given her an idea of what kind of present he was hoping she would help him find. "You said you needed help finding a present for Jackson, is it for Christmas, his birthday or something else?"

Grandpa Jack smiled at her. "Something else."

Jackson was happy when the meeting was over. Jim walked the new client to the door as he passed Victoria's desk he glanced at the flowers. She had received another bouquet yesterday. They still looked good. He wanted to throw them out. There was still no indication as to who had sent them. He walked around to Sasha's side of the cube. "Will you tell Victoria to come see me when she gets back to her desk?"

"Yeah sure. Victoria should be back soon. She's been gone pretty much since your meeting started."

"Really?" She hadn't told him she was leaving the office for anything today. He was in the sales meeting for almost two hours.

"I think she said she was having lunch with someone."

Sasha smiled and added, "Maybe it's with whoever sent the flowers."

Jackson didn't like the sound of that. "Maybe." He said walking into his office. He sat down and pulled out his phone.

Jackson: "Where are you?"

Victoria: "On my way back to the office. Why?"

Jackson: "You've been gone for nearly two hours?"

Victoria: "I'll make the time up. I'm getting in the car. I'll be back in a half hour."

Jackson didn't send another message. He knew that they couldn't talk about it in the office, at least not the things he was concerned with. He didn't care if she made the time up or not. He wanted to know who she was with and why she had been gone for two hours. Even as he worked, he kept an eye on the clock until she knocked on his door.

"I'm back. I'm sorry I was gone so long. Like I said I will make up my time." She didn't wait for a reply she went to her desk. Her text alert went off.

Jackson: "Who did you have lunch with?"

Victoria: "A friend."

Jackson: "What's this friend's name?"

Victoria: "What's with all the questions?"

Jackson: "Why won't you answer my questions?"

Victoria didn't want to deal with this now. She was still thinking about her conversation with Grandpa Jack, and she needed to get back to her work. Sasha poked her head over the wall. "Did you have a good lunch?" She asked wiggling her eyebrows up and down.

"I had an interesting lunch with a friend." Victoria had been about to say with a nice man but realized that Sasha would make more of it than it was.

"A friend huh? Is it a friend with benefits?" Sasha said suggestively.

"No. Sasha I know you mean well, but can you just keep your nose out of my personal life for once." Victoria knew she sounded angry, but she didn't care. She was tired of Sasha's nosiness and interfering. Sasha sat down with a thud and all her teasing stopped. The entire office was eerily quiet. Victoria didn't realize that she had spoken loud enough for everyone to hear.

Jackson approached Victoria's desk. "Can I speak to you in the conference room for a minute."

Victoria sighed heavily. "Sure." She got up and strode quickly down the hall with Jackson following her. She pushed the door to the conference room open and went inside. She didn't sit down. She stood with her arms folded over her chest.

Jackson waited until the door closed firmly. "What's going on?" He moved closer to touch her, but she backed away from him. "My bad. I know we're in the office. So, what was that about, out there?"

"It's nothing." She said looking down at the floor.

"Does it have anything to do with your mysterious lunch today?" He asked restraining himself from pulling her into his arms. She was apparently upset about something, and he wanted to hold her and tell her that he would fix it.

It had everything to do with her mysterious lunch. Grandpa Jack asked her to be his great grandchild's baby Momma. That was a mouthful, and it was crazy. He wanted her to intentionally get pregnant with Jackson's child. When he first said it, she thought he was joking, and she laughed. She quickly came to understand that it was no laughing matter. He was serious, and she sat there listening to him explain why she should go through with it.

Thanks to Grandpa Jack she kept envisioning a child with Jackson's blue eyes, a mixture of their skin tones and curly hair being held by Grandpa Jack. The crazy part was, she had pretty much ruled out the possibility of having children of her own a long time ago. She was getting older every year and eventually she wouldn't be able to get pregnant. Victoria shook her head. "No. It has nothing to do with lunch. I think it's just P.M.S.." she said avoiding his eyes.

Jackson didn't believe her, but it was clear that she wasn't going to tell him what was bothering her. "Why won't you tell me who you had lunch with?"

"It was just a friend. Why are you being so inquisitive about it?"

Jackson stuck his hands in his pockets. "Sasha said you had a date."

Victoria rolled her eyes. Was he jealous? "If you're jealous, don't be. While I did have lunch with a man today, he is not trying to get in my pants, of that I'm sure."

Although they were in the office, he pulled her into his arms and kissed her tenderly. She tried to push him away, but his arms were like steel bands around her. He nibbled her lips until she kissed him back. He wanted to continue kissing her, but he finally let her go.

"I need to apologize to Sasha." She said pulling out of his arms.

"We'll continue this tonight." He said before she left him.

She was right when she said he was jealous. He had never experienced this before. He'd never been the cave man type, but then he'd never cared enough for a woman to be upset at the thought of her with someone else. Hearing Sasha say that she was on a date made his blood boil.

The thought of someone else holding her hand and touching her in any way made him feel out of control. Jackson watched her walk out of the conference room. Something was bothering her, and he intended to find out who or what it was.

# Chapter 12 Losing Control

Victoria had climaxed multiple times, and still, Jackson was trying to coax another orgasm from her. He held her hips as he ground into her slowly. He licked the side of her neck then whispered in her ear, "I want you to cum again for me." She didn't know if she could, but as he began to thrust into her again, she felt the tingle deep within that said she was going to.

Jackson slid his arms under her shoulders. He kissed her fiercely, as he felt her hotness gripping his cock as she came again for him. Jackson ripped his mouth from hers when the pleasure of her body pushed him over the edge. He slammed into her squeezing his eyes shut as he lost control. "You're mine Tori," he said fiercely in her ear

Victoria lay with her arms still wrapped around Jackson. He was heavy on top of her, but neither of them had the strength to move. Jackson moved off her but pulled her close as he closed his eyes and fell asleep. She lay there staring at the ceiling for a few minutes. This time had been different. Their sex had always been hot and passionate, but this time Jackson was different. She didn't know how to describe it. He seemed more aggressive than before.

Victoria slid out of bed and stood to look at him. He was laying on his side, his hair still damp with sweat, clinging to his face. She thought she was imagining it, but his hair had seemed to be getting lighter. It almost looked dark blonde instead of the brown it was when they first met. Her eyes traveled downward. His chest rose and fell evenly. He was deep in sleep.

She was staring at his midsection. The hair here was dark blonde. "The carpet doesn't match the drapes," she whispered. He hadn't removed the condom. Even soft, she was impressed with him. She gently extracted the condom and tossed it out before covering him up. He didn't move a muscle. She went into the bathroom, closed the door and turned on the light.

Jackson had texted her before she left work to go home and pack a bag because he wanted to spend the night with her. She had been surprised when he sent her the name and address of the Omni Hotel. He explained that with his grandfather staying with him that they couldn't spend the night at his place and he didn't want to go to her house for the same reasons.

It was a beautiful suite. Victoria started the water in the huge marble tub, adding lavender scented oil and bubble bath. He had met her in the lobby and had already checked in. He took her straight to their room. Jackson ordered room service while she took in the view of Dallas from the floor to ceiling windows. She didn't spend a lot of time in hotels, but Victoria knew that this room had to be expensive. Other than not having a kitchen, it was like an apartment with its own balcony off the living area, dining area, huge bedroom, and bathroom.

After they had eaten, Victoria stood looking out the window into the night. Jackson could see that she was still distracted. He walked up behind her wrapping his arms around her waist. Jackson pushed her hair aside kissing her neck. He spun her around and kissed her lips gently pushing her against the glass. He undid the buttons on her top, pushing it down her arms to slide to the floor, he undid her bra allowing it to join her shirt at their feet. He placed feather light kisses down to her shoulders before sucking each nipple into his mouth. He loved the sounds she made. The slight hitch in her breath as he flicked his tongue over the harden brown nubs, the moans when he sucked them into his mouth made his cock hard as steel.

He found the button and zipper on the back of her skirt and undid them as he kissed the soft flesh of her stomach. He felt her hands on his shoulders as he pulled her skirt and panties off at the same time. He looked up inter her eyes briefly as the material reached the floor. He kissed her thighs before he grabbed one leg raising it to drape it over his shoulder. He rubbed his lips against her pussy, inhaling her scent.

Victoria trembled in the tub thinking back on what he had done to her in front of the open window where anyone could see them. She hadn't cared at the time. Victoria giggled to herself. She had never been this wanton in her life. She sighed and closed her eyes. She thought about her conversation with Grandpa Jack. He had to have some mental problems to suggest that she get pregnant with Jackson's child all because he wanted great-grandchildren before he died.

Now that he had put the thought in her head she couldn't help herself from picturing what a child from Jackson might look like. What kind of relationship would she have with Jackson if she was the mother of his child? Would he want to get married? Would she, for that matter? How would they work out a co-parenting situation? Would the baby be with her all week and with him on the weekend? What if he wanted to have sole custody?

"Stop that." She said out loud.

"Stop what?" Jackson asked entering the bathroom. Jackson came in and stood by the tub beautifully naked.

"Nothing," Victoria said trying not to stare at him. How on earth had she ended up here? A few weeks ago, all she wanted was to rest and watch a movie in her sweats, but now she was in a luxury hotel with a hot guy who made her toes curl.

"Scoot forward," Jackson said moving to join her in the tub. Victoria slid forward, and he slid behind her. He pulled her back to lay against his chest. "This is nice." When he woke to find himself alone in the bed, he thought she might have left, but then he saw the light coming from the bathroom.

They sat in the tub for a little while before Jackson took the body wash and they washed each other. He got out and then helped her out, rubbing her body dry with the sizeable white bath sheet. He had a hard time standing still as she did the same for him. By the time she had finished, he was hard again. She allowed him to apply lotion to her body. He took his time enjoying the fact that she was getting turned on.

He took her from behind while they faced the mirror. When she closed her eyes, he softly said, "Look at yourself." She opened her eyes. "See how beautiful you are to me." He touched her full bow shaped lips. She opened her mouth sucking his finger. "So beautiful." He ran his hand down her throat, massaged her breasts, then pinched her nipples as he thrust into her. "My beautiful Victoria."

He continued to move his hand down until he reached the apex of her thighs. She met his eyes in the mirror as he rubbed her clit. Her breath caught in her throat and her inner walls began to pulse around him. She closed her eyes as she came. He thrust harder and faster and held on tight as she came again causing him to cum too.

In the next week Jackson finished his evaluations, and after a few more meetings with Peter, he spoke with the Human Resources director at Quinn Enterprises giving her instructions for each employee of Albrecht Armor. Even though he had officially finished the evaluations, Hank reminded him that until the paperwork was finalized, he still couldn't tell anyone about the deal.

Jackson wasn't pleased about it, but he knew he couldn't tell

Victoria yet. She was still behaving oddly. Victoria had been out for a few more long lunches and insisted that it was either a friend or personal errands. She was distracted by something. When he asked her if something was bothering her, she told him it was nothing, but he knew better.

On the day Hank called to say that Jackson and Peter would come to the office and sign the contracts Victoria called in sick. Jackson hadn't seen her the night before because Grandpa Jack had decided to go home. Jackson insisted on driving him even though his grandfather had said he would hire a car to take him back to the estate.

When he got into the office, Millie told him that Victoria had called in sick. He went to his office, closing the door. He called her from his cell phone. The phone rang until it went to voicemail. He left a message asking her to call him. He hadn't heard from her by lunch. He called again. This time it went directly to voicemail. That meant the phone was turned off. He tried not to think about it.

He was worried about how tomorrow was going to go. He had set up a town hall to tell everyone in the office about the deal he and Peter had made and later in the afternoon he was holding a press conference at Q.E. to announce the acquisition of Albrecht Armor. He was worried about Victoria's reaction to the news. He had made sure that everyone was being offered a position or compensation if they chose not to accept the offer of employment that he proposed. He had created a post especially for Victoria.

Victoria sat in her living room with her mother. "What are you going to do?" Helen asked from her spot on the couch.

Victoria was pacing back and forth. "I have to think about it a little longer before I make a decision." She knew she didn't have long. Sasha had texted her earlier to see how she was feeling and told her that Peter had some big announcement he was making the next day. She was going to see Jackson tomorrow, and she would have to talk to him.

She had avoided talking to him all day. When he called in the morning, she had been in the bathroom and missed the call. When he called later, she had turned her phone off on purpose.    She realized that she didn't want things to change between her and Jackson. She liked things the way they were.

"You're going to wear a hole in the carpet." Her mother said. She stopped pacing.

"I'm going out for a bit," Victoria said grabbing her keys and a jacket before heading out the door.

Victoria turned her phone back on an hour later while she sat in the park near her house. She had two voice messages from Jackson and several texts. She wasn't ready to talk to him, but the last message he had sent indicated that if she didn't call or text him soon that he was coming to her house.

Victoria: "Sorry, I took some medicine that knocked me out for most of the day, but I'm feeling better. I'll be back to work tomorrow."

Jackson: "Good, you had me worried.
I'll bring you and your mother dinner."

Victoria: "No, I just want to sleep some more.
Momma has already made me some of her famous chicken soup. I'll see you tomorrow at work."

Jackson finally agreed not to come by, and Victoria felt like she could breathe again. She still wasn't sure what she was going to do, but she at least had more time to think about it.

She felt like she was losing control of her life. In the space of a few weeks, everything had changed.

# Chapter 13 Going Public

"Are you ready for this?" Hank asked as he entered Jackson's office at Q.E.

Jackson stood and slipped his suit jacket on, fastening the button. He said, "As ready as I'll ever be."

"Beth is staying here to make sure that everything is ready for the press conference this afternoon. Christine is going to meet us downstairs."

Jackson proceeded to walk out of the office followed by Hank. He looked like himself in the black Armani suit, light blue shirt, and dark blue Christian Lacroix tie with matching kerchief in his left breast pocket. He was wearing his Cartier watch and cufflinks as well as his monogrammed signet ring. His dark blond hair combed neatly in place. The only thing missing was the beard that he had shaved off almost a month ago, but he didn't quite feel like himself.

During the limo ride to Albrecht's office, Christine, his head of Human Resources ensured him that she had followed his directions with each of the employee offer packets which were sitting in the seat beside her in a large box. Jackson was only half listening. His mind was elsewhere.

He was thinking of Victoria and how she would react to the news he was about to give. He had wanted to see her last night, but she insisted that she wanted to rest and that she would be at work the next day. He knew how important her position was to her, but he hoped that she would be happy with the position he had created for her at Q.E.

She would be paid well and have a position of authority, a position that would allow her to grow and offered the potential for her to become so much more. As the car turned into the parking lot of Albrecht Armor Jackson tried to clear his head of the worries that were plaguing him.

Victoria stood looking at herself in the mirror. She was wearing her hair pulled back today. She had thought of wearing it down, but with it pulled away from her face she felt more confident, more professional and today she would need to hang on to that professionalism. Sasha came in. "I don't know what the hell is happening today, but Jackson just got here with some other people and he...," she paused. "is smoking hot."

Victoria listened as Sasha described how he looked and described the other hot guy and a lady that came in with him. "They went straight to the conference room. Do you have any idea of what's going on?"

Before Victoria could answer, Millie, stuck her head in the lady's room. "Everyone is going to the conference room. You two better come on." Victoria, Millie, and Sasha fell in line behind the others as they went down the hall. Victoria was the last to enter the conference room. She moved to the opposite end of the room from Jackson, Peter, the unknown lady and the man who stood together. Jackson did indeed look incredible.

Jackson watched her as she entered, moving to the far side of the room. She had her hair pulled back, the way she wore it when they first met. She dressed in a lovely black velvet dress that clung to her curves. Her heels matched the texture of her dress.

Peter cleared his throat and spoke first. "I'm sure you all are wondering what is going on? You all know I took on the responsibility for Albrecht when my son died a year ago. From the very beginning, I intended to sell the company." There were sighs and murmurs from everyone in the room. "As I got to know you all I found myself between a rock and hard place. I couldn't allow all my son's hard work and yours to be for nothing. Over this year I realized that I don't have it in me to run this business as it should be. The man standing next to me," he indicated Jackson. "is Maximillian Quinn of Quinn Enterprises. He has made an offer to buy Albrecht Armor, and I have accepted." Again, there was whispering and sounds of shock around the room.

Jackson was watching Victoria's face as Peter spoke. She had taken a couple of deep breaths, but beyond that, he couldn't measure her response. Jackson talked to everyone. "Peter has made a tough decision, but I want you all to know that his number one concern has been for the well-being of each of you. As part of our deal neither of us could speak of the agreement and for one month I had to work with you all. The purpose was for me to get to know you so that I could find positions in Q.E. for you.

Christine has an offer packet for each of you. My lawyer and partner Hank has confidentiality agreements that each you will need to sign whether you accept the jobs I'm offering you. I will be holding a press conference this afternoon to announce the acquisition of Albrecht Armor by Q.E. formally, but until that announcement, you will be bound by this agreement. "We'll give you all a chance to look at the packets. If you have questions now is the time to ask." Christine and Hank passed out the packets and confidentiality agreements.

Victoria had her arms folded across her chest. She wasn't looking at him. She was talking to Sasha, Sam, and Millie. There were a few questions asked as they looked at the packets. Hank and Christine answered most of them. He watched as she opened her package. Jackson couldn't tell from her facial expression if she were pleased or not. He watched as she used the pen offered to her to put her signature at the bottom of two of the documents. He knew one would be the confidentiality agreement. The other could be the offer of employment or the compensation agreement if she weren't accepting the job offer.

Victoria scribbled her signature on the bottom of the documents before stuffing them back into the envelope and handed them back to the lady he called Christine. Sasha and Millie watched as she gave the envelope away. "That was fast. I guess your offer was pretty good." Millie said.

Victoria watched as Jackson made his way towards her. When he reached her, he said quietly, "Can I speak to you alone?"

Victoria realized that Sasha, Millie, and Sam were all listening and tuned in to her and Jackson. "Can't this wait?"

"No." He said taking her hand and pulling her out of the conference room.

Once they were in the hallway, she pulled her hand from his. "What do you want Jackson? No, wait, your name isn't Jackson, it's Maximillian or should I call you Mr. Quinn?" She asked quietly.

"Jackson is my name. It's my middle name. I wanted to tell you, but I couldn't. I know that you're probably angry with me."

"I was angry with you last week when I learned who you were," Victoria said.

"What? How?" He asked shaking his head confused.

"Grandpa Jack told me." She answered, then continued. "He wasn't bound by your confidentiality agreement apparently. The day I took the two-hour lunch after the first flowers came, I had lunch with your grandfather. He told me that he wanted me to help him with a present for you. That's why I went to lunch with him."

"I don't understand. A present for what and why would Grandpa Jack tell you?" Jackson said rubbing his chin.

"I didn't understand either until he told me what he wanted as a present for you." She smiled at him. "Which at first sounded even crazier to me than you masquerading as someone else. I like Grandpa Jack, but I think he may be a little nutty. The present he wanted my help with, is a baby."

Jackson looked as shocked as Victoria when she first heard it from Grandpa Jack. "A baby?"
She told him the rest.

"Your grandfather has baby fever. He thinks that you and I could give him a great-grandchild before he dies. He was hoping that if he told me who you are, that I might be more inclined to forgive you when all this came out. Not because you're filthy, stinking rich, but because he thinks that you are in love with me." Jackson just stood there staring at her. She didn't want to hear him say that his grandfather was wrong, but she knew Jackson couldn't be in love with her even if she were in love with him. Victoria turned going back into the conference room. She needed to get away from him before she blurted out how she felt.

Jackson stood still as Victoria walked away. His grandfather was right. He did love Victoria, and the thought of her carrying his child made his heart pound wildly in his chest. He followed her into the conference room. She was standing among her friends talking as he purposefully walked to her. He took her face in both his hands looking her in the eye. "Grandpa Jack is right. I do love you, Victoria."

Victoria stood dazed as Jackson's mouth lowered to hers. His kiss was slow and filled with fire as he nibbled her lips and caressed her tongue with his. Her arms went around him as she gave in to the desire burning in her.

When Jackson pulled away from her smiling, he repeated it.

"I love you."

Sasha whooped and clapped beside her. Victoria realized what had just happened. Jackson had just taken their relationship public.

After the meeting ended and everyone was out of the conference room Sasha and others wanted Victoria to explain what had just happened. Victoria didn't want to share her relationship with everyone. She told them only that she and Jackson were seeing each other for a little while. When they wanted to know if she had known who he was, she just said that she was as surprised to find out as they were, which wasn't a lie.

Jackson, Christine, and Hank came out of the conference room. Hank carried the box containing all but one of the employment packets. Jackson had a large envelope in his hand, and he approached Victoria. "We need to talk about this."

Victoria was working on emails; she didn't look up because she knew what he was holding in his hands. "There's nothing to talk about."

"Why are you turning down the job offer. I created this position for you." Jackson said spinning her chair around so that she would look at him.

"That's exactly why I can't take it." She knew that Sasha, Sam and anyone else in earshot was listening. "Can we discuss this in private?"

He grabbed her by the hand and took her into his office closing the door behind them. "Why are you turning down the opportunity of a lifetime?"

"I don't want to be the one everyone is talking about. I don't want to be the woman who got the job because she's sleeping with the boss."

"That's not why I'm offering you this job, and you know it," Jackson said shaking the envelope at her.

"I know that, and you know that, but that's not what others will think. Besides I have accepted a job offer already." Victoria said sitting in the chair in front of his desk.

"What do mean? What job?" Jackson said standing over her.

"After your grandfather told me who you are, I got to thinking, and I realized that if you and I were going to continue to see each other that I couldn't work for you. I started sending out resumes, and I've been interviewing on my lunch breaks."

Jackson turned moving around the room. That's why she had been going to lunch and coming back late. Victoria wasn't seeing someone else as he had thought. She was looking for another job. All of this is why she had been so distracted.

"I received two job offers, and I've finally made a decision. If you check your email, you will find my letter of resignation."

Jackson stood with his back to her. He wanted her to work at Q.E. He knew that she was smart and capable, and he wanted to make sure that she moved forward into a position that she would love and thrive. She stood and wrapped her arms around his waist. "What company's offer did you accept?"

"Look at me," she said turning him by pulling on his arm. She gave him a peck on the lips. "If I tell you, you have to promise not to pull some 'Fifty Shades of Grey crap and buy the company, okay?" She chuckled as she said it, but the truth was he could afford to do just that, and they both knew it.

He didn't want to make that promise, but he did it anyway. "I promise." He looked at his watch. I have to get back to Q.E., but tonight you will tell me everything." He kissed her. "I will send you the address to my place, bring enough clothes for the weekend." He left, and Victoria went back to her desk.

Victoria stepped out of the elevator on the forty-fifth floor of the building where Jackson lived. The concierge had used his passkey to allow her up. Directly across from the elevator was the entry to his penthouse. Before she could knock, the left side of the double doors opened. "Miss. Timmons, please come in." A lovely Hispanic lady said. Victoria entered. "I'm Maria, Mr. Quinn's housekeeper. I'll take your things."

Victoria removed her jacket and handed her the overnight back she was carrying. "Thank you."

"Mr. Quinn is in his office. He said for you to join him in there." Maria pointed to a door behind her.

Victoria crossed the marble floor and softly knocked as she opened the door. Jackson was on the phone, but he smiled as he saw her. She closed the door and looked around the room, trying not to listen in on his call. His desk sat in the corner of the room facing away from the wall of windows behind it. Victoria would have turned the desk the other way, but then she would probably never get anything done, looking at the view. It was dark out, and the lights of the city lay beneath them like jewels.

While he talked she walked around the room. There was a television mounted on the wall surrounded by shelves with books. She read some of the titles. He had books by Jane Austin, Mark Twain, J.D. Salinger, Emily Bronte', and Harper Lee, just to name a few. There were photos and other items placed here and there. She was looking at a picture of him, and the man named Hank and two blond women in ski gear on a snow-covered mountain when he ended the call. He came around the desk and kissed her lips, cheeks, and forehead. "I'm so glad you're here." He kissed her lips again enjoying her sweetness. "Are you hungry? I'm starving."

He took her by the hand and led her out of the office, through the living room, past the longest dining table Victoria had ever seen and into the kitchen. The apartment had an open concept. From the wall of his office, you could see clear across to the wall behind the kitchen, and it seemed like it was half the size of a football field.

Most of Victoria's house could fit in this space. All the furniture was white or cream colored. There were no blinds or window coverings at all in the living room. The windows were floor to ceiling and nearly from one end of the apartment to the other.

In the kitchen he let her go long enough to grab oven mitts and pull covered plates from a warming oven beside the stove. He set them on the bar and uncovered them. "I had Maria cook up one of her delicious meals for us." He took the covers off.

"Wow, this looks and smells great," Victoria said sitting on a stool in front of one of the plates. She could barely see the edge of the plate. There was a large piece of pot roast with potatoes and carrots, soft rolls and asparagus. Jackson got two wine glasses and set them next to their plates before disappearing around a corner behind the kitchen wall. He returned with a bottle of wine. He poured a glass for each of them before joining her at the bar.

She took his hand; they bowed their heads as she said a

prayer. When she finished, and they had started to eat, Jackson spoke. "Now will you tell me about this job offer."

"I accepted it." She said taking a bite of her roast. It was tender and juicy. "This is wonderful." She said as she chewed the food. "I accepted a position at E.G.S."

Jackson wanted to be happy for her, but he wasn't. "Electronic Gaming Systems? What will you be doing there?" he asked poking at a potato.

"I will be the Director of Customer Relations. Essentially, I'll be doing the same things I've been doing at Albrecht. I will have to get familiar with all their products before I start working. After Thanksgiving, I'll be going to Los Angeles for product training." This was the part of the conversation she had been dreading.

"Los Angeles, for how long?" He asked putting down his fork and picking up his glass.

"A few weeks, maybe longer."

Jackson didn't say anything, he drained his glass. Thanksgiving was in a few days. He didn't want her to go, he didn't want her anywhere but with him. "Well, I guess we should make the most of the time we have together then." He pulled her from her stool and led her up the winding staircase that started by the front door and down the hall to his bedroom.

Jackson sat on the side of the bed next to Victoria. He had been watching her sleep for a few minutes. She lay on her stomach with her face turned towards him. Her hair was a mess of curls all around her head. The cream-colored sheet barely covered her bountiful brown bottom. She had one leg out from under the cover. He smiled to himself. She belonged here in his bed. He leaned over and kissed her shoulder, then her cheek. "Wake up baby. It's time to get up."

Victoria groaned and swatted at him. "We just went to sleep." He continued to place kisses on her back moving lower. When he tugged the sheet from around her lower half, she opened her eyes. "Is that why you woke me up?" She asked as he slipped his hand between her legs.

"Yes." He said as he kissed each cheek. Jackson climbed on the bed. He pushed her knees apart with his. Victoria arched her back raising herself off the bed. Jackson entered her thrusting deep. Yes, she belonged here, he thought. In my house, in my bed. He gripped her hips driving deep. Victoria grabbed the bed sheets bracing herself for each thrust. Jackson loved the way she felt. She came in no time, with him following her.

Victoria and Jackson showered together and found their way down to the kitchen. Maria had prepared breakfast for them. Fresh fruit and peanut butter and jelly stuffed waffles. Victoria realized that she could come to love Maria easily. After eating, Jackson went into his office for a bit. He told her to make herself at home.

She called her mother to check in with her. "Hi Momma, is everything okay?"

"Yes."

"Do you need anything?"

"No. I'm fine. How're things with Mr. Moneybags?"

"Pretty good, but you wouldn't believe this apartment. It's so big that most of our house will fit on the first floor."

"Wow. That's pretty big. Did you tell him about the job yet?"

"He took it well, I think."

"I gotta go, honey. My show just came back from commercial." Victoria disconnected the call.

Victoria explored Jackson's home. The first floor had a lovely bedroom and private bath just past the kitchen, not to mention two half bathrooms. Victoria hoped she had not wandered into Maria's private space, but the room didn't look like it housed any personal belongings. Near the door to that bedroom, she found two different doors that led outside. One to a small patio with an outdoor sofa and chair, and the other to a rooftop pool with a garden on the other side. Upstairs there was a workout room with every machine she had seen in a gym. There was a steam sauna, game room with every game console on the market and a wall of games, three full baths and three bedrooms and that didn't include the master suite with a closet bigger than Victoria's bedroom.

She still hadn't seen where his housekeeper had disappeared to, but when she came back down, there were two covered dishes on the counter. She uncovered one and found a chicken salad sandwich on whole wheat bread sliced perfectly with chips and a pickle. Jackson saw her in the kitchen eating. "Sorry about that. I didn't intend to take so long."

Victoria wiped her mouth. "No problem. I got lost wandering around this place. It took me a while to find my way back to the stairs." Jackson laughed as he bit into his sandwich. "Seriously though, is Maria a witch or something. I haven't seen her all morning, but I come down, and this is sitting here. It's like she just appears out of thin air."

Jackson smiled and pointed to the corner cabinetry on the other side of the kitchen. There's a door on the side of that wall that leads downstairs. I bought one of the apartments on the floor below and had an elevator put in. She lives downstairs because I wanted her to be available at all times."

"You're kidding me, right?" Victoria stared at him in disbelief.

"No."

"She can come and go as needed." He said as he finished his sandwich.

"She does get time off occasionally?" Victoria asked.

"Of course, she has two days a week off, usually Monday and Tuesday."

"Tell me what you think of the place." He demanded as he took their dishes and placed them in the dishwasher.

"It's okay." She said scrunching her face up.

Jackson leaned across the bar and kissed her. "Just okay?"

"Yeah, it's okay. I don't understand why a single man needs all this space and it seems a little impersonal to me. I'd guess you hired a decorator and this is the result of someone not knowing you well. It's beautiful, but it's boring."

"You would decorate it differently if you lived here?" He asked coming around pulling her off the bar stool and leading her to the living room.

"Yes, I would, but I don't have to look at it every day."

"You could look at it every day." Jackson said pulling her into his lap. Did she hear him correctly? To Victoria, it sounded like he was asking her to move in with him. When she didn't say anything, he added, "Would you like to look at it every day?"

"Are you asking me to move in with you?" She stood moving to sit in the chair next to the sofa.

"Yes, I am." Jackson watched as Victoria bit her bottom lip. He was hoping she would say yes.
That she wanted to be with him as much as he wanted to be with her.

"Jackson, that's a really big step, and we haven't known each other long. I have my mother to think of, and I just bought my house." Victoria's head was spinning.

Jackson had thought of all those things. He got on his knees in front of her holding her hands. "I know this is a big decision, but I want you here with me. There is plenty of room for your mother, and you can sell your house or keep it."

Victoria sat shaking her head. She didn't know what to say. Victoria hadn't even said that she loved him yet. She did, but they had only known each other a month. She wasn't ready to live with him.

Jackson wanted her to say yes, but he could see that she had to pick it apart before she could see that this made sense. "You don't have to decide right this moment. Think it over and let me know when you're ready. Take all the time you need." He kissed her.

# Chapter 14 Thanksgiving Dinner

Jackson arrived to pick Victoria up for Thanksgiving dinner with his family around two in the afternoon. He rang the doorbell. A few minutes later the door opened, and Jackson finally got to meet Victoria's mother, Helen. She was half a foot shorter than Victoria, but he could see that she had the same curvy figure. She wore leggings and a t-shirt that he was sure Victoria gave her. It said 'I'm not short. I'm fun size.'

"You must be Jackson." She said when she opened the door. "Come in. Victoria will be out in a minute."

Jackson spoke before sitting down near the door. "It's a pleasure to meet you, Mrs. Timmons."

"Call me Helen."

Victoria finished her hair and double checked her make up. She was nervous. She wanted to look nice for her introduction to Jackson's family. She had straightened her hair, something she rarely did. She was wearing a red dress that had short sleeves and a high collar with matching red high heels. Victoria's make up was simple and natural except the red lipstick that was a shade darker than her dress. She grabbed her purse and her leather jacket.

When she entered the living room, Jackson was laughing, and her mother was standing close to him. "What's going on in here?" Victoria asked curiously.

Jackson spoke while still laughing. "Your mother wanted to know what I looked like." Victoria knew that meant that either her mother had asked to feel his face with her hands or she had gotten eyeball to eyeball with him using the little bit of vision she had to look him over.

"He's tickled pink because I said, there was no denying that he was white, but at least my Vicky picked a looker."

Jackson started laughing all over again. It was one of the best compliments he'd ever received. "Thank you, Helen."

Jackson was still laughing as they walked to the car. Victoria hated leaving her mother alone on Thanksgiving, but her mother had insisted on staying home. She felt more comfortable in their home where she knew where everything was, and she could move around without bumping into things or having to use her cane.

"Your mom is very outspoken," Jackson said smiling at Victoria.

"Yes, she is. She says that she has lived long enough to be able to say whatever she wants." Which she did all the time, but Victoria couldn't ever remember her mother not saying what was on her mind. She could be very diplomatic when necessary, but she never held her tongue.

"I wished she had come to dinner with us. I think she and Grandpa Jack would get along famously." He said still smiling.

Victoria had stayed with Jackson until Sunday morning. He kissed her goodbye at the elevator after asking her and her mother to join him at his family's Thanksgiving Day dinner. Victoria, knowing her mother well, told him that Helen would not attend, but that she would be delighted to have dinner with his family.

Once she got home, she did extend his invitation to her mother. "Jackson has invited us to have Thanksgiving dinner with his family." Victoria stood next to her in her mother's bedroom. Helen was sitting in her usual spot in front of the television.

Helen smiled at her daughter. "Is that so? No thanks. I'd rather stay here." Helen knew she didn't have to explain it to Victoria. She understood that her mother didn't like being around others because of her lack of vision.

"I told him that you would say no, but I wanted to let you choose for yourself." Victoria left her mother and went to her room.

Victoria had been surprised when she and Jackson walked out of her house. He wasn't driving the Taurus, which he explained as they turned away from her home, belonged to his grandfather. He had picked her up today in a car that was very low to the ground and very sleek. She didn't know what it was until she asked, but to her, it looked like an alien spaceship. He told her it was a Lamborghini Veneo.

"Do you like it? I could get you one for Christmas." He said, knowing she would say no.

"No thank you. I like driving. I don't need to fly everywhere, besides I'm sure it's super expensive." She said as he seemed to be flying by every other car on the road.

"This one goes for nearly five million, but we could get you something else. What kind of car would you like?" He asked taking her hand in his.

Nearly five million, she thought. That's crazy. The amount of money Jackson spent on this car would support her and her mother for the rest of her life. "I'm fine with my Lancer, thank you very much." She laughed. She tried to put the thought of how much money he'd spent on the car out of her head, but it stayed in the back of her mind. It seemed crazy to spend that kind of money on a car. She could buy every house in her neighborhood and have money left over.

As he exited the highway and drove to his family estate, they talked about the other cars that he owned, the properties and boats. She was a simple girl, could she get used to his lifestyle? Jackson watched her face as they turned down the narrow road leading to the gated entrance of the estate. She was in awe. "This is where you grew up?"

"Yes. Mom and Dad bought this place when I was young. The house wasn't as big then. They've made additions over the years. Grandpa Jack lives in one of the guest houses on the property." Victoria realized that he had said one of the guesthouses. How many could there be?

Jackson explained to her that as his grandfather got older, his mother insisted that grandpa Jack sell his house and live with them here. His grandfather insisted on having his own space away from them, so they moved him into his own house built on the property.

Victoria realized she was out of her element as Jackson explained that the house sat on twenty-five acres. They paused at the gate long enough for Jackson to push a button on his visor. The gate opened, and they had passed through it. She still couldn't see a building. Down the long winding road, she began to see a structure. They crossed over a bridge with a river running under it. Jackson explained that there was a pond and a stream as well as a wooded area, tennis courts and a stable among other things.

As they got closer the building, it turned out to be a huge home, correction, mansion with a significant water feature in the middle of the drive. There were two other cars parked out front, both foreign and expensive.

Jackson got out and went around to help Victoria out of the car. As they walked up the stone steps to the door, Victoria tried to take it all in. The house was incredibly beautiful. Jackson led her through the wrought iron double doors opened by a tall, thin older man wearing a black suit. Of course, they had a freaking butler. "Happy Thanksgiving

Thomas," Jackson said as they entered the house.

The man smiled. "Happy Thanksgiving to you as well, Mr. Quinn."

"Thomas this is Victoria Timmons, my girlfriend," Jackson said removing his jacket.

"It's a pleasure to make your acquaintance Ms. Timmons," Thomas said with a slight bow.

Jackson helped her out of her jacket handing it and her purse to a woman in a maid's uniform who appeared as if by magic. "Welcome home Mr. Quinn. Everyone is in the drawing room."

"Thank you, Cindy," Jackson said slipping his hand in Victoria's taking her down the hall. Just beyond the archway, they passed a broad winding staircase. They continued beyond another arch and turned left. Victoria was in awe of the majestic nature of the house. They passed several rooms before reaching the drawing room. She was only able to catch a glimpse of them as they walked.

The drawing room was beautiful and elegant. In the center of the room sat a light blue sectional sofa with a chaise on one end. Across from the glass coffee table were three chairs in a cream color with side tables between them. At one end of the room, there was an oversized fireplace. Victoria's mother could easily walk right into it without hitting her head. Above it was a family portrait, no doubt hand painted by someone famous in the art world. At the other end of the room was a modern looking bar with tap on one end. Victoria also took in the white baby grand piano between the sitting area and the bar.

"Max darling, you're finally here." A tall, blond older woman said coming towards them with her arms open for a hug. It would take Victoria a while to get used to hearing people call him Max. To her, he would always be Jackson.

Jackson hugged her and then said. "Mom I'd like you to meet Victoria Timmons."

"It's a pleasure to meet you, Mrs. Quinn," Victoria said with a smile.

"Call me Kelly." She said hugging Victoria. "Come in, let me introduce you to everyone." She took Victoria's other hand pulling her away from Jackson. Victoria was introduced to Jackson's father, Doug, who was handsome and tall like Jackson. Jackson got his coloring from his mother. They had the same blonde hair and blue eyes.

"Hi, we haven't officially met yet. I'm Max's best friend, Hank." He said extending his hand to her.

Victoria shook his hand. "Nice to meet you, Hank."

"Victoria, I'm Elizabeth, Max's sister. Everyone calls me Beth." She smiled warmly at Victoria as she greeted her.

"This is my father, Jackson. I think you two are already acquainted." Kelly said indicating Grandpa Jack who had been sitting near the fireplace.

"Hello beautiful." He said as Victoria went to him. She bent down and hugged him so that he wouldn't have to stand up.

"Hi Grandpa Jack. How is the leg?" She asked when he let her go.

"It's getting better every day." He said then added in a whisper. "I'll be glad when the cast comes off, so I can go back to my house." Victoria laughed. She was happy to see him. He put her at ease.

They sat in the drawing room for a while talking and

exchanging pleasantries. Jackson, Hank and his father were at the bar deep in conversation, probably discussing business. Victoria sat with Kelly, Beth and Grandpa Jack.

Victoria liked Jackson's mom and sister. They weren't anything like what she expected after seeing their vast wealth. They both seemed down to earth and relatable. Jackson's mother wanted to know everything about Victoria and Jackson's romance.

Victoria was delighted when Thomas appeared informing them that dinner was ready. They made their way to another section of the house to the dining room. Victoria and Jackson walked behind the others with Grandpa Jack. He was maneuvering well despite the crutches.

The dining room looked like something you would find in a movie. It had coffered ceilings with pendulum chandeliers made of hundreds of crystals, floor to ceiling windows on two sides of the room with a magnificent view of the garden. Jackson informed her that this was the small dining room. Victoria was shocked to learn they had more than one.

Jackson's father pulled out his wife's chair before moving to the other end of the table. Victoria saw cards indicating who would sit where. She and Jackson were seated side by side near his mother. His grandfather sat on the other side of the table across from her. Beth and Hank sat on either side of Jackson's father.

Dinner was delicious, and the conversation was pleasant. The group mostly talked about Jackson, Beth, and Hank and how the three of them were trouble makers as children and teenagers. They asked Victoria about her childhood. She told them that she had never given her mother a moment of worry. She explained that her father traveled a lot and that with her mother's loss of vision that she had to be very responsible at a young age, but her mother had encouraged her to have fun and experience life.

She did have some funny stories for them as well. She told them about the time a friend in school asked her to take care of his pet crab while he was away at summer camp for two weeks. Victoria would occasionally put the crab on the floor and allow it to walk around instead of being stuck in its glass bowl. It had wandered out of her room, and her mother thought it was a tissue lying in the floor and when to pick it up, but it started moving, and she screamed threatening to make seafood gumbo out of it. They all laughed but thought it very amusing that the crab's name was George D. Crab.

Overall Victoria felt the day had gone well. After dinner and dessert, they made their way back to the drawing room for a while. Jackson's mother fussed over her father, and when he'd finally had enough, he asked Jackson to help him back to his bedroom so that he could rest. Grandpa Jack kissed Victoria's cheek before he left. "I'm glad you came, darling."

"I am too." She said smiling. Beth and Hank had disappeared as well. Jackson's mother went with him to help her father get settled for the night.

Jackson's mother left him and his grandfather alone after she was satisfied that he had everything he needed. "Today was a good day." Grandpa Jack said leaning back on the pillows.

"Yes, it was. I think everyone had a good time." Jackson agreed.

"When are you going to propose? She's the one, and you know it." Grandpa Jack said smiling.

Jackson did know it, but he knew that Victoria wasn't in the same place. Jack always took what he wanted, and that was not going to work in this case. He was utterly in love with Victoria. Until she was ready, he had to sit back and be patient.

"Open the middle drawer and get the box that's in there." Grandpa Jack said.

Jackson crossed to the dresser, opened the drawer and took the ring box back to his grandfather. "Open it." Grandpa Jack said. Jackson opened it. It was his grandmother's engagement ring and band. It was a simple gold ring with a small diamond and a plain gold band. "It's not much, but I want you to give it to her when you propose."

Jackson fingered the ring in its simple black box. "It's perfect."

"I carried that ring in my pocket every day for three years, and when I could give your grandmother everything she deserved, I asked her to marry me, and she said yes. We were happy. It wasn't always easy, we fought and went through our share of tough times, but we did it together."

Jackson closed the box, slid it into his pocket and hugged his grandfather. "Goodnight Grandpa Jack."

Jackson's father offered to show Victoria the garden. She walked with him through the house and outside. "We have several gardens, but this one is my favorite." He said strolling with his hands behind his back. Victoria looked at the various flowers, trees, and bushes. The path was lit by lamps that made everything look very picturesque. They walked in silence. He led her through a maze of hedges stopping in an area of statues and fountains with long benches.

"I can see why my son cares for you. You are charming and beautiful." Doug said as they walked. "He's like me in that respect. We can recognize beauty in all its forms."

Victoria smiled, "Thank you."

He moved closer to Victoria stroking her face gently with his finger. "Your skin is so soft." His father moved towards her as if he were going to kiss her.

"Are you serious right now?" She backed away from him. Jackson's father was hitting on her and not in the cute way his grandfather had. This was downright creepy.

Victoria sat in the car looking out the window as they left his parent's house. She was still in a daze. She couldn't believe what had happened. She told him to go to hell. She found her way back to the house. She became frustrated when she couldn't find Jackson. She found Thomas hovering near the grand staircase and asked him to get her things and to let Jackson know that she was ready to leave.

One of the maids had just handed her her jacket and bag as Jackson, and his mother came towards her. "Is everything okay?" Jackson asked looking at her face. She was upset.

"I need to get home." She said sliding her arms into her jacket. Thomas appeared with Jackson's jacket. She waited patiently while he said goodbye to his mother. "Thank you for having me, Mrs. Quinn."

"You are welcome." His mother replied.

Jackson looked at Victoria again. He had asked her again if something was wrong once they were in the car. She assured him she was fine. He wasn't convinced, but he didn't want to upset her further by continuing to ask. She didn't say anything during the ride back to her house.

Victoria closed her eyes. How could Jackson be related to that asshole? She took a deep breath trying to calm her nerves. Her life had been so simple before Maximilian Jackson Quinn showed up at her office. She sat in the passenger seat analyzing everything from that day until now. She knew she should tell Jackson what his father had said and done, but why would he believe her. She would just keep this to herself and make sure that she was never alone with his father again.

She climbed out of the car before Jackson could get around to her side. "Baby, what happened tonight? Everything was fine and now..."

She interrupted him, "I'm just tired. That's all." She kissed him briefly and unlocked the door. "Goodnight Jackson."

Victoria closed the door. Jackson stood there looking at the door as he heard the lock click into place.

Jackson had tried to convince Victoria to go Christmas shopping with him on Friday. She told him she did not under any circumstances want to spend the day getting pushed and shoved around by thousands of people trying to get Black Friday deals. Something was still off, but Victoria had promised to spend the night at his house, and he would enjoy as much time with her as he could before she left on Sunday for California.

She had arrived just before sundown, and they sat on the patio watching the sky change colors like a live work of art behind the Dallas skyline. She hadn't said much since she had arrived. Victoria sat with her bare feet in his lap. It was cool out, so Jackson rubbed her feet to keep them warm. When the sun finally disappeared, and the light was gone, they went inside to eat the dinner Maria had made for them. Jackson was sad that she would be gone for three weeks. He couldn't imagine what he would do with himself while she was gone. After dinner, he led her upstairs and made love to her again and again until they both fell asleep.

Victoria rolled over reaching out for Jackson. She opened her eyes when she realized she was alone in the bed. She stretched and got out of bed. She walked through the room that Jackson called a closet to get to the bathroom on the other side. Maria had hung her jeans and shirt up and had placed her other items on the center tabletop. Her shoes were tucked neatly beside Jackson's. She went into the bathroom, emptied her bladder and started the shower.

She was still trying to find a way to tell Jackson that his father was a lecherous asshole. She hadn't stuck around to hear what possible explanation he might give for his behavior. She walked away from him and found everyone in the drawing room.

Jackson's father entered the room shortly after Victoria returned. He didn't say anything to her. He joined his wife on the sofa. Kelly wanted to know what she thought of the garden.

Victoria told her it was lovely. She watched Jackson's father sitting with Kelly. He seemed so devoted to her. Victoria thought that maybe she had misinterpreted his actions. She tried to push those thoughts out of her mind as she dressed and went to find Jackson.

Jackson opened the front door to find Teegan standing there holding a chubby blond-haired baby. When the concierge had informed him that she was there, he had been stunned. They hadn't seen each other in a little over a year. "Um, come in." He said moving aside so that she could enter the apartment. "What are you doing here?" He asked closing the door behind her.

Teegan sat the baby on the sofa and pulled his outer clothes off. "I'm here because I need help." She said removing her own jacket. "We need help," she added picking up the baby. "Max, I need help raising our baby."

Jackson was sure he had heard her wrong. "Our baby," he said looking at her and the child in her arms.

"Yes. I know I should have told you about Christian as soon as I found out I was pregnant, but I..." She stopped talking as she looked past him.

Jackson turned to find Victoria standing on the stairs. Victoria turned going back up the stairs. "I'll be right back." He said to Teegan as he dashed after Victoria. She was in his bedroom.

"Tori, I don't know what she's talking about, but I intend to find out." He said as he closed the door. She was standing by the bed. He crossed the room and put his hands on her shoulders. "Look at me, baby."

Victoria met his eyes. "That's your baby? That's what she said."

"Yes, that's what she said. I need you to have a seat and let me find out what the hell is going on, okay." He said gently pushing her to sit on the bed. He kissed her forehead. "Just hang out here while I find out what is going on."

Victoria closed her eyes tightly, took a deep breath and said, "No. I want to hear this with my own ears." She stood and went to the door. Jackson followed.

# Chapter 15 Being A Quinn

Victoria was ready to go back home to Dallas. Her product training was complete. The staff had been great to her as she learned all about the gaming consoles and software that worked within the systems. Most of them were a lot like the guys at Albrecht, smart and goofy. They played around while working and that was how they came up with ideas and improvements to the product line.

They had given her an office, but Victoria had insisted on sitting amid the programmers. From that moment on they had treated her like she was one of them. They invited her to lunch and made sure to include her in Friday night's happy hour. Greg, the head programmer seemed to be sweet on her. He brought her sweets from the bakery down the street every morning. He lingered around her desk throughout the day to chat with her. He always told her how beautiful she looked.

On the last day of her stay during the goodbye celebration they threw for her, he asked to speak to her alone. They stepped away from the others.

"I know you are leaving to go back to Dallas tomorrow and I should have manned up and done this earlier. Victoria, I like you, and I was wondering if you would consider keeping in touch with me once you get home?"

She was flattered. A few months ago, she would have considered it seriously. Greg was tall and handsome. He was smart and hardworking, but she knew that it would never work. She loved Jackson, and she didn't see that changing. She smiled. "Greg, you are sweet, and if I weren't in love with someone else, I would want to keep in touch with you."

"He's a lucky man," Greg said before he joined his friends on the other side of the room. She sighed thinking, that Jackson probably would disagree with Greg.

Victoria stopped by the front desk to see if she had any messages. The hotel that EGS had arranged for her to stay in was near the production design facility which meant she hadn't wasted any time stuck in traffic. She had a rental car, and since she was leaving to return to Dallas tomorrow, she would turn it in at the airport in the morning.

It was hard to believe that she had been in California for three weeks. Even though there was probably not going to be any snow in Dallas, at least it felt a little like winter. It was too warm for her here. She couldn't imagine being here for Christmas.

In her room, Victoria showered and got comfortable in her sweatpants and a large t-shirt. She called her mother after she ordered room service. She missed her, and she wanted one of her mother's hugs, several of them she thought. They talked for a while. Her mother told her that Jackson had come to the house. Victoria wished he would just move on. It would make it so much easier for her if he did.

Jackson had tried calling and texting her every day since Teegan told him about the baby. She should have blocked his number or something, but it made her feel better knowing that he hadn't entirely given up on her, even though she knew that it was over.

She sat thinking back to her last day with Jackson. When they returned downstairs, Teegan sat on the sofa breastfeeding the baby. Jackson introduced Victoria to her. "Teegan this is Victoria, my girlfriend."

Teegan tried to cover the look of shock on her face, but Victoria saw it. Victoria sat in the chair across from her.

Jackson stood beside Victoria's chair with his hand on her shoulder. "Teegan, what is this? If that is my child, why wouldn't you tell me?"

"We had been broken up for a month or so. I didn't intend to keep the baby, but I was raised Catholic, and I couldn't have an abortion. I planned to give the baby up for adoption, but once he was born, I couldn't do it. I've been living off the money I made modeling, but that's not going to last, and I need help."

Victoria felt sick to her stomach. She knew that Jackson would take care of his child financially, but she also knew that he would want to be a part of his life. What did that mean for the two of them? She had never imagined that she would get involved with someone with a baby momma situation. She also knew that she could not make Jackson choose between her and his child. Could she be involved with him and not be involved with his baby with another woman?

The sound of knocking brought Victoria out of her depressing recollection of the last moments she spent with Jackson before telling him that he needed time to deal with his present situation and that she needed time to decide if she wanted to be involved any further in his life.

Victoria stepped in front of the hotel door and peered through the peephole. She was surprised by who was on the other side of the door. She opened it. "Mrs. Quinn, what are you doing here?"

Mrs. Quinn smiled. "We need to talk."

Victoria moved aside and allowed her to enter the room. She closed the door. "Please have a seat."

Mrs. Quinn sat in the chair across from the love seat that Victoria sat on. "I'm here to bring you home. My son is miserable, and I'm pretty sure that you are too."

"Mrs. Quinn, it's over between us," Victoria said with a deep sigh.

"I know that you broke off your relationship with my son because of Teegan and the baby. Jackson told me that you said that he needed to be there for Teegan and the baby. It's a noble, but a stupid thing you did." She stood and walked around the room while she spoke. "I've been doing stupid things since the day I met Doug. One of them was thinking he was the best I could do, but I'm telling you, you can't do any better than my son. He was willing to accept Teegan at her word about the baby. Hank, Beth and I were not.

We insisted on a paternity test. That's when the truth came out. When Teegan realized that once we knew the truth, she would never get what she was after which was money. She told us everything. My husband Doug has been having an affair with her for some time now, it started while she was dating my son." Kelly stopped moving and looked at Victoria. "Doug is the baby's father. Of course, Jackson insisted on the test to be sure. Doug didn't deny any of it and said he was happy that it was all out in the open." Jackson's mother sat next to Victoria.

"A few weeks ago, my soon to be ex-husband got caught by some photographer coming out of a hotel room with a woman. We couldn't see who the woman was, and he wouldn't tell us, Jackson was fed up with it. He cut him off financially after he found out that he was paying for an apartment and car among other things for this woman. The woman he was caught with was Teegan. She figured if she couldn't get any money from Doug, she'd get it from Jackson."

Victoria tried not to cry. She had sobbed every day for the past three weeks, but tears rolled down her cheeks. Mrs. Quinn reached out wiping her face. "Being a Quinn woman isn't going to be easy. There are going to be times when the two of you will disagree about things, there are going to be times when people are going to try to separate the two of you. If you're going to be a Quinn, you are going to need to develop a thick skin. You already have a strong will. Any woman who can stand her ground with my son is worthy of the name Quinn. Victoria, my son, has changed since he met you. I've never seen him as happy as he has been since you've been in his life. He loves you. Do you love him?

Victoria was choked up and couldn't speak. She nodded her head. Mrs. Quinn grabbed her hugging her tight. "Then the only thing we have left to do is pack your things."

"My flight doesn't leave until tomorrow night," Victoria said once she was able to speak.

Mrs. Quinn laughed and pulled back to look at Victoria. "You have so much to learn. Quinns don't fly commercially. We have our own jet. Well, we have a few. That's another thing about being a Quinn, you will want for nothing." She grabbed Victoria's hand and led her into the bedroom.

Jackson didn't know what else to do. He had called, sent text messages and flowers to her daily. He'd even gone to her house. He was miserable without Victoria in his life. Every day he thought of her. He wanted to hold her and tell her how much she meant to him. He wanted to kiss her and make love to her every chance he got.

He told himself that she had made up her mind and that there was nothing he could do about it. He looked out the window of his bedroom remembering the way she looked laying in this bed sleeping after he had made love to her all night. He realized that he would never be happy again without her and he wasn't going to let her walk out of his life just like that. He got up and went into the bathroom. He hadn't left the apartment for a few days, and he needed to get cleaned up before he went to find her and change her mind. He always got what he wanted, and he wanted Victoria.

While he was dressing Maria informed him that his mother was on her way up, a surprise. He pulled on a pair of jeans, a white button down and a dark blue pullover knit top. He ran a brush through his hair and splashed on some cologne before putting on dress socks and sliding his feet into a pair of black loafers and went down to meet his mother.

His mother stood in the living room pacing. She didn't look like herself. She always wore a suit or elegant dress. Her hair styled to perfection, and she never left the house without her face being made up. Today she didn't have any makeup on. Her hair was pulled back in a ponytail, she was wearing a red sweater and skinny jeans with red boots. "Mom, is everything okay?"

"Everything is fine, or it will be." She said smiling at him. She reached out touching his cheek. "I'm divorcing your father." She said with a huge smile. Before Jackson could speak, she went on. "I should have done it a long time ago. I'm sure you have lots of questions, but we can save that for another time. I know that Christmas is just a few days away, but I wanted to give you my gift now. Stay right there she said and walked past him to the front door.

Jackson turned and watched as she stood aside, and Victoria came in. Before he knew what had happened, she was in his arms, kissing him. He picked her up off the ground returning her passionate kisses. She was here in his home, in his arms, kissing him.

When they finally pulled back from one another, he pressed his forehead to hers. "You are the best present I could ever hope for."

He looked around and realized his mother had slipped out the door. "I'm dying to hear how you ended up here with my mother."

Victoria promised that she would tell him, but she wanted to give him the best kiss he would ever have. He swung her up into his arms and carried her upstairs to his bedroom. They undressed each other slowly. When they stood naked before each other, Victoria pushed Jackson backward until he fell back on the bed. She kissed his chest slowly working her way down his body. She took his length in her hand licking the tip of his cock. She took him into her mouth.

Jackson moaned rising to watch as Victoria worked her mouth up and down the length of him. Watching her beautiful mouth sucking the life out of him made him want her more than ever. He wouldn't last too much longer like this. He pulled her away. "Come here." He said picking her up and placing her on her back. She wrapped her legs around his waist as he settled between her thighs. She kissed him passionately as he entered her forcefully. He pushed into her, loving the feel of his beautiful, sexy woman. He grabbed her by the hair pulling her head back exposing her neck.

Victoria moaned as he licked and sucked her neck. He moved faster, pounding her harder. "Don't ever leave me again! Say you belong to me. Tell me that you will never leave me again" He grunted in her ear.

"I belong to you. Only you. I'm not going anywhere ever. I love you Jackson" She told him, closing her eye as her release gushed from her. Jackson continued thrusting until she came a second time, then he allowed himself to go over the precipice to join her in bliss.

# Epilogue

"They did it?" Millie asked. She was on the phone with Sasha. She hadn't been able to attend the wedding. Her new granddaughter had come a week early.

"They did it. It was a beautiful ceremony. You should see this estate, and it's freaking huge." Sasha said watching the happy couple having their first dance.

"I hope you are taking lots of pictures. I can't wait to see them." Millie said bouncing the baby in her arms. "I have to go, but I'll expect those pictures soon. Tell Victoria and Jackson congratulations from me."

"Will do," Sasha said disconnecting the call. Brian put his arm around her. "They look happy." She said laying her head on his shoulder. She watched Victoria and Jackson dancing.

Victoria pulled Jackson off the floor and over to Sasha. "Isn't this wild?" She asked Sasha as they watched her mother, Helen dancing with her new husband. Grandpa Jack dipped Helen and kissed her. They were happy. Victoria wiped the tear from her eye.

"Are you crying again?" Jackson asked grabbing her by the chin to steal a quick kiss.

"I can't help it. Who would have thought that your grandpa and my mother would fall in love and get married, not to mention that they got married before we did?"

"That's your fault. You're the one who doesn't want to waddle down the aisle." He said rubbing her ever-expanding belly. He couldn't wait to hold their first child. Jackson would marry her anywhere, anytime and she knew it. They had joked about it. He told her that as long as they were together, she could have what she wanted.

# Available Now

# About the Author

Kimberly Smith was born in Aurora Colorado in 1970. She was raised in Dallas Texas by her mother along with her siblings. Her first experiences with creating fiction began with Barbie and Ken romances. It was not long before she introduced conflict and complications into the lives of her dolls. She started reading romance stories as a teenager and has created fascinating stories for years entertaining her family and friends with her creativity.

# Coming Soon
## What You Are
## The Wreight Relationship

# Connect with Me

**https://www.kimberlyreneesmith.com/**

**https://www.facebook.com/creativekrs/**

**https://www.twitter.com/CreativeKrs**

**http://www.instagram.com/creativekrs**

Made in the USA
Coppell, TX
26 August 2020